The Letters

Peter Carpmael

Copyright © 2018 Peter Carpmael

All rights reserved.

1st Paperback Edition 2023

Previously published as a Kindle ebook

The font used is Arial

Navigation: To help you find your way around this book, the page numbers on odd numbered pages are followed by the total number of pages in the novel:

'1 of 112'

Even pages give the number of the current page and the number of the first page in the next chapter :

'Page 2   Next Chapter starts on Page 22'

Front Cover by Joanne Bradley

Contents

Introduction

Chapter I: To Halt Bridge	Friday	1
Chapter II: Murder	Saturday	22
Chapter III: George Investigates	Sunday	33
Chapter IV: Burglary	Monday	51
Chapter V: Mr Griefly's Letter	Tuesday	64
Chapter VI: Grenade	Wednesday	86
Chapter VII: George Tells the Tale	Thursday	109
About the Author		113
First page of the original manuscript		115
Other Books by Peter Carpmael		117

INTRODUCTION

When Lieutenant Peter Carpmael's war came abruptly to a close at Monte Cassino in the summer of 1944, it must have been like the end of a long dream in which his life had hung suspended. For years afterwards the sands of the Sahara bled from the binding of his copy of the *Pickwick Papers* just as the fragments of shrapnel embedded in him after the mortar explosion continued working their way up through his wounded body. Recuperating in a Scottish hospital his mind was alive with the after-shocks, the indelible memories of a campaign in a distant theatre of war followed abruptly by enforced and indefinite home leave.

That's where we left it in the Preface to Peter Carpmael's early children's book *The Magic Chatty*, composed in the immediate post-war period, followed by its sequel *Upon the Other Side* in the mid-to-late Fifties. But there was one even earlier survival, a manuscript preserved on the backs of brittle war-time teleprinter sheets, which takes the reader straight to that period of recuperation in 1945, Peter Carpmael now on crutches minus his right fibula, visiting friends in the much-loved North-East and the villages just inland of Tyne-side.

The Letters is set in a quite different tradition to the later Narnian-style semi-dreamworld of the children's books which followed it. This time the genre is detective fiction, but with the unusual twist that the author appears firmly embedded in the story, accompanied by characters whose real existence is only lightly disguised. Peter's contemporaries would have had little difficulty in recognising who was who.

Peter himself is the young officer on leave, having "stopped a small package in an encounter with the Boche", as if his life-threatening wound had been no more than a sticking-plaster job. The leading investigator, "George" repeatedly referred to in such admiring tongue-in-cheek terms as "the great man" whose "gems of oratory" radiated the "benevolence of his personality" was clearly something of a local character, the structure of whose social life rested squarely upon Opening Hours.

A standing joke in *The Letters* is the influence exerted by the ubiquitous public-house which dominated rural life in the mid-1940s with its dismal nightly call of Last Orders followed inevitably by Closing Time: *All about us was a general scraping of chairs, a shuffling, a rustle of clothes; mugs made their miserable last clatter; and farewells sounded on all sides mingling with goodnights.*

As with the children's books, Peter Carpmael's eccentric fondness for punctuation (particularly the amphibious semi-colon) is unblushingly on display, and this is highlighted even more emphatically by his delight in how real people actually speak and in the quest to do justice to it. Speech, after all, owes next to nothing to punctuation: *"My word," said George with feeling, "this air's got some pep, what? Pah! – delightful!".... "Yes, Peter I have been thinking – I have an idea, an idea, which came to me – this morning, Peter man! together – you and I – we'll track down the murderer."*

What makes *The Letters* peculiarly engaging is that it is so unashamedly "of its time". The social life is all-consuming, with its Mrs Cranfords perpetually brewing tea, domestic items, crockery, heavy winter coats, and even more specifically the war-time necessities:

Suddenly realising that it was after black-out time, we scurried round putting up pieces of paper, pulling curtains, and generally concealing all lights from view outside – less from the Boche than P. Stott, the local Constable. The sound of the steps was by the door as we completed the rushed operations – was it George or the Constable?

And yes, of course, that ultimate tradition of detective fiction, PC Stott, the bumblingly self-important representative of the law: *There was a long silence. P.C. Stott stood very still, holding his bike in front of him. At last he spoke: "I advise you gentlemen not to*

Introduction

meddle in matters which you are not qualified to look into and wasting my time with your talk!" He jerked his head vigorously to indicate that the discussion had come to an end; and trundled his bicycle on up the hill.

The mainspring of narrative interest here is first established on Peter's arrival in Hentham. A prosperous-looking gentleman with a prominent paunch confides just as the train draws up at the platform: "There's no good in the air – just you see…" And sure enough everything is set up for the mysterious death of Jane Griefly and the various leads picked up ineptly by the accident-prone Stott and with increasing conviction and excitement by the magnificent George and his admiring Watson, young Lieutenant Peter.

The author was, of course, an admirer of John Buchan whose ingenious romantic fiction produces such portentous personalities as Sir Walter Bullivant in *The Thirty-Nine Steps* and Laputa in *Prester John*. Peter Carpmael's narrative is studded with a series of delightful Buchanesque pen-portraits designed to lead or mislead the reader as the crime genre demands. One passing instance among many: *a most inspiring figure with the portly frame of a Greek merchant, the scarlet face of an English brewer, and a long white moustache, which could only have been grown by a man of the Victorian era.*

The "Letters" of the title are of course central to the ingenuity of the final unveiling of the culprit, and there is a satisfying sense of artistic circularity to the outcome and the inevitable discomfiture of PC Stott. Above all, Peter's own presence defines this book, and even as he lies in bed on his first night of leave, relishing the luxury of a real English adventure, the dream-like setting of his later children's books is already very much in evidence: *Could this really be true? I was almost afraid to sleep. Instead of the Cranfords and the Thompsons, might I not waken to the Libyan scrub, or to the tossing of the Hospital ship? Still pondering, I dozed off into a Fairyland of happy dreams.*

Patrick Carpmael, 2023

CHAPTER I: TO HALT BRIDGE - FRIDAY

It was a Winter's evening; and with the dusk came a chill. I was cold although I wore a thick army great-coat, but my spirits were aglow. I hurried onto the pavement out of danger from the taxis, and then into the security of the station itself. The dirty station walls, the gloomy station entrance, the wretched station officials with their slouching walk and their unapproachable expressions, looked gay to me; people stood waiting, dejected, forlorn; soldiers packed with equipment beyond recognition staggered up the many flights of stair-cases, their boots ringing out a clatter, as they went from pillar to post misguided all the while; Air-force officers with caps at a jaunty angle, and glamorous maidens attached to crooked arms sped through the jostling crowd; everybody moved amidst platforms, policemen, slot-machines, and miserable passengers. I looked at the tired faces; and they looked contented. I saw the waiting groups; they chattered brightly. I glanced towards the big clock; it shone and sparkled with a hundred dancing lights. Even Newcastle station on a cold November night when a dirty yellow mist was coming from the Tyne outside, when all was grimly depressed, to me looked dazzling; I was home again. This was England.

Shaking myself from my dreams, I walked briskly towards the ticket office, apologised for hitting an old man with the helmet attached to my respirator, and lined up to buy my ticket. After a long wait I reached the head of the queue. An agreeable stout gentleman standing in front of me commented slyly on the weather, intimating that he knew something most people did not. With nothing better to do I became drawn into a long discussion on enemy aircraft, of their ability to fly in weather such as this, of the chances of our obtaining our tickets before we should be imperiled was very enlightening. I *was* very enlightened; and I'm sure he considered me highly intelligent, for I listened murmuring "Aha" with necessary variations of voice intonation, until the line indeed ended.

The Letters

I was surprised to hear the large man ask for a single ticket to Halt Bridge, for this was to be my own destination; but discreetly making no mention of it, I was relieved to see him pick up his ticket and change, raise his hat, and disappear into the whirl-pool of scurrying men and women.

I clambered into my train which moved off punctually at five o'clock into the grey night, past the shabby Tyne-side buildings and factories, slowly chugging forward out of the station. I was very happy – same old, dirty coaches, same Victorian pictures, and advertisements here and there obliterated by A.R.P. notices, whose corners hung dejectedly; the racks with their torn netting, the shaded blue light in the grimy ceiling, the filthy cushions, all represented my nostalgic thoughts of the past eighteen months. There below was the River Tyne, winding stately through the changing green of the countryside. I was free; I was happy; it was England; and now, all about it that meant so much to me was very near. The train shuddered onwards, stopping every so often to belch a gush of bodies on to a platform, then to suck in a fresh series of tumbling creatures; I watched it all with the interest of a child taken on his first trip, fascinated by the stations, enchanted by the green of the grass and the leafless trees bunched in squares upon the hillsides.

It was not until we had nearly reached Hentham that I stared away from the window into the gloom of the carriage to study the occupants: over in the corner an old lady, knitting khaki mittens, opposite her, a young man in dirty overalls, his eyes shut, his mouth open, next to him a large man with a tweed suit – a large man (I looked again, indeed it was the man to whom I had conversed at such length by the ticket office), a pretty girl of eighteen years, sitting between him and me, and facing me was a C.M.P. Corporal.

I was just congratulating myself on escaping identification by the large man, when the surly town of Hentham leered up at us out of the shadows; the train pulled up with a shriek, and a concussion, which dislodged my respirator from the rack to the floors with a great noise, causing some considerable confusion and

Friday

commotion in the compartment; everybody looked from the Corporal to myself with eyes so ferocious that I wished myself back in the deserts of Libya – but thought afterwards how very rash I had been. Everybody, the fat lady, the pretty girl, the large man, and the young man in overalls who had been wakened from his sleep, uttered expressions of horror, commenting on "somebody's" carelessness, and on the "danger" of such an occurrence. The pretty girl suddenly realised this was Hentham at the same time as the people outside came to realise this was the Carlisle train, with the result that I received many a muttered oath, many a petted speech as I ignominiously groveled to retrieve my fallen articles; the Corporal wanted to leave the carriage too, but he stayed to give me assistance. A laden Corporal helping a sheep-like officer, an impatient pretty girl with umbrella and case waiting to get out, a couple of baleful glares from the fat lady and the large man, a scornful, mocking glower from the young man, and excited chatter from a surging body of three women attempting to enter, this was the dreadful situation in a nut-shell.

With a muttered apology and a red face, I replaced my delinquent haversack upon the rack, putting the blame in my own mind on the English railways in not making a luggage-rack suitable for my respirator. I sat down, and was finally humiliated by the pretty girl, who strutted off with a parting word, which concluded with emphasis on the added "sir" looking glumly at the Corporal, who withdrew in a dignified manner; then the bulge of bodies outside exploded inside, and the compartment became filled with women laden with tins, and butter, and baskets, and a hundred and one other purchases. I prayed that the train would not move off yet, not until they had settled; and my prayer was answered. There were only three of them, but their conduct recalled to me George Cranford's famous words: "they were all talking at once, but there was nobody listening."

I wanted to see the darkened, lovely valley of the Tyne between Hentham and Halt Bridge, but Kismet had ordained that I should once more be confronted with the large man in the tweed suit, so I was neither startled nor distressed when loudly addressed by a voice which claimed my recent acquaintance. I looked back into the squalor of the compartment; noticed four fat women now sitting opposite; quivered inwardly; perceived the mocking face of the overalled young man; saw the large man; and behaved as though I had failed to see him previously. Within a few minutes he was lecturing to me, this time on his personal history, pieces of which floated to me above the tidal rumble of the four fat women (the original lady had joined her fat voice to the rest, expressing herself quite as volubly as any of the others). Thus when he at last enquired about my own past, I had acquired the following information: he was a Mr. Jack Bromley, who had lived in Halt Bridge for over twenty years, and what he did not know about the Tyne valley, I gathered, was not worth knowing; he kept a newspaper shop; he was married, having three children; he was quite content, though not with the government's promotion of the war, or its effort; and he sincerely expressed the opinion that we had met somewhere before, though he could not recall where.

It was to this last remark that I replied first. I tried to be concise, but the large man delved into my clipped phrases enquiring intimately about the most obscure incidents, until my tale was enlarged to his approval. I told him that I was in the Buffs battalion, which had been stationed in Halt Bridge some two years earlier, that I had bought many a morning paper from his shop, and that my name was Peter Cadogan. He recalled vividly, he said, qualifying his statement by assuring me that my fiancée, Sheila, was in the best of health, an assurance which made my heart beat faster. When I mentioned my recent return from Egypt, his eyes protruded from their sockets, and his manner altered as that of an individual who attending a sick pig sees it magically change into a prince; merely by saying the word "Egypt", a word mysterious in the ignorance of the layman's mind, I had become a hero. In this false lime-light I nervously gave an account of myself, of eighteen months spent between Egypt, and the Libyan desert, of wounds received, which originated the sick leave on which I was now embarking with the Cranfords at Halt Bridge.

Friday

Mr. Bromley leaned forwards tapping me on the knee in a fatherly manner: "You'll not find Halt Bridge what it was when you left. Just lately there's been things abroad that's not been hereabouts before. You just see." He nodded his head slyly, as he had done on Newcastle station.

Although I could feel the train slowing down, though I could see by a side-glance through the steamed-up window the stone grey bridge crossing the Tyne, which meant the end of my journey, though I got to my feet, slung my haversack across my body, vainly adjusting my cap, I was tempted by Jack Bromley's words. I asked him:

"And what is this change in the village?"

The train came to an erratic stand-still. I stumbled forwards and out of the carriage.

Mr. Bromley was handing over his ticket to the collector, as I reached his side. To remind him of my expected information, I repeated my question.

He looked at me quickly, and before disappearing hurriedly into the dusky street, said, "There's no good in the air. Just you see."

Wishing the porter a good-night, and presenting him with my ticket, I slowly walked through the swing gate, thinking whilst I waited for the level-crossing gates to open about the words "There's no good in the air" – what did he mean? Surely drowsy Halt Bridge was not veiled in mystery? The train chuffed my thoughts aside, and with the familiar clang of the gates there returned to me all the suppressed emotion associated with my arrival. I walked briskly across the line and turned left down the path beside the railway. Soon I came to the house to which Sheila had been evacuated from Newcastle with her family.

I was elated, happy. Sheila did not know I was back. What a surprise! What a wonderful evening! How picturesque the

The Letters

skeleton trees were, silhouetted against the darkening sky! How sombre everything was! Yet how fresh! My mind made black white, and white gold. I turned the last corner to see before me once more the square, grey building which I knew so well. There was an orange glow by the Cranford's sitting room – so they were at home.

The reunion after so long a parting was such as occurs infrequently in a life span, and when we had stopped being excited Mrs. Cranford swept out of the room. She would make some tea immediately, she said. Within a moment she was back again with a kettle of water. She put it onto the red coals of a fire, which I had only once seen absent in that grate – once, when Sheila and I had been left in charge, when it had for reasons of inattention gone out; it was lighted again – not by the combined operations of Sheila and I, but by Mrs. Cranford some hours later with a glib distribution of sugar upon the coals, and a lighted match; this was a phenomenon which never ceased to astonish me.

As a white cloth, assorted crockery and utensils clinckled onto the table with unbelievable speed as sundry choice delicacies appeared upon the plates, Mrs. Cranford glided to and fro talking to me, unravelling the news of twenty months in a most remarkable way, as though hers was a long-prepared oration. Her anecdotes, her comments, and her information were interspersed with ejaculations relating to my visit.

"Ee!" she said, "Fancy!" or sometimes, as a variation, "Ee, Peter! Fancy this!" or perhaps, just, "Ee-ee –"

Within the first few minutes of our meeting, I had been told that, "Sheila is away, Peter. What a great shame, isn't it? She and Wendy have gone to spend a week with an aunt of theirs in Scotland. Oh dear, they only left yesterday." I was upset, but I knew this was only a "putting off", for we were bound to see each other very shortly. When Mrs. Cranford learnt that I was staying in the area, she was all for rushing out to cable her daughters' immediate return. However, I pointed out that little Wendy would be enjoying herself, that it was a long, tiresome journey, that the two had only

Friday

just arrived, and that finally the relation immediately concerned might be offended at so sudden a withdrawal of the delightful Cranford children. We compromised in a mutual decision to consult George (that is to say Mr. George Cranford, previously referred to in this story) for his philosophic and unbiased opinion backed, as it was, by a wisdom gained in years of unscrupulous business life.

George apparently had not yet arrived for his usual weekend, but was expected "any minute now". My hair bristled, for his very name brought back memories of the days when "in our cups" together we discussed at great length the depth of meaning behind his revealing statement concerning we officers of the Buffs regiment (referring to those subalterns of the battalion who were constantly entertained by the two families of Thompson and Cranford, whose hospitality was as profound as the sincerity of their friendship) "were like ships, which pass in the night"; of the days when brains battled, as we endeavoured, before the hour of three o'clock on Sunday mornings, to show that Napoleon and Hitler were common scoundrels, that Churchill was the only man worth talking about; this he did with numerous irrelevancies, and incidentals dealing with the price of pork, and the relative merits of poached and fried eggs; of the day that he made his monumental speech at the cottage, a speech made in that chilling voice, shaking with emotion, word by word deliberately spoken, with considerable emphasis laid upon those words, which he believed to be most important – it was a masterpiece, and had Churchill written it himself, he could certainly not have read it as convincingly as George spoke that night. (What the speech was about, I'm afraid I can't remember, but then weak is the mind of youth, unable to concentrate upon the products of so fertile an imagination, so great an intellect. Sad am I that those gems of oratory are lost to me for ever!)

Mrs. Cranford urging me towards a chair by the fire instantly whisked tea, accompanied by some of the copiously filled plates of edibles, in my direction. I sat warming myself by the ruddy patch of coals in the midst of yellow flames, nervously encouraging her to sit

The Letters

beside me, rising to attempt to serve her with tea, and being remonstrated for my efforts. Abashed I sat down once more, remaining silent until asked a multitude of questions: was I staying the night? What exactly was my position at the moment in relation to the Army? and what had I been doing with myself? It was the moment I had feared, for I knew what a lot of explaining I had to do. However, exhorted by a radiant smile from Mrs. Cranford, I cautiously stirred my tea, sipped it, and began.

"Well. After rummaging about in the desert for long enough, I was sent back home a) because my unit was being relieved, and b) because I had stopped a small packet in a small encounter with the Boche."

Mrs. Cranford was violently affected by this news; and she interrupted me:

"But Peter, are you all right now? are you quite well?"

I assured her that everything was as it should be, but she eyed me suspiciously as I continued, "We had a grand trip back, and landed recently in a Northern port. It was cold compared to Egypt, you know, but we were all so happy to get out of that beastly country with its sun and its flies. When I went to a Newcastle hospital, I was wrapped up in bags of sweaters to keep the cold out."

Mrs. Cranford signified her sympathy by intermittent clucks. I had reached the difficult part of my tale; I believe her feminine intuition, or whatever it is that makes Mothers know things without thinking about them, or studying them at all, made her realise this was the vital part of my words, for she leaned forward expectantly in her chair.

"Well," I began again rather glumly, "I was told at the Hospital that I could – well anyway – they said – well, the M. O. Thought I needed a rest, and –"

"What you mean to say," broke in Mrs. Cranford with a kind

Friday

smile, "is that you've got some leave, and may you spend it here? Oh, Peter, you can stay as long as you like."

Wretchedly I said, "Thank you very much, but the M. O. said I couldn't go further away from the Hospital than fifty miles, because that was their ruling with leave cases who were to be re-admitted, so –"

"You can stay as long as you like, Peter, you know that. I'll go, and tell Mrs. Taylor now," she said.

"No please don't do that yet," I pleaded, "you see I've got a fortnight's leave, and won't that be rather an imposition?"

"That will be lovely Peter," was her quick answer. "But what about your Mother? Does she know you're in England?" she added.

"Oh yes, I cabled on landing, and told her the exact position – that I would stay at the Blaydon here. And I asked her, and Pop – who of course wouldn't come – to come up, and stay while I had what they called 'rest leave'."

Mrs. Cranford exclaimed, "You silly boy! You stay here. Mrs. Taylor will let you use Tommy's room, I'm sure."

"Thank you, Mrs. Cranford," I murmured lamely, "and if I am to stay for a fortnight, then it won't be necessary to go to all that bother of bringing Sheila back here, after she's just gone to Scotland. It's a long journey, and expensive."

Mrs. Cranford smiled, "Anybody would think you didn't want to see her."

"With you here why should I worry?" I said facetiously.

We laughed. Mrs. Cranford refilled our cups with tea, and plied me with cakes, and rolls, and buns, and jam, and apologies for not attending to me before.

"I wouldn't think the war had been going on for two years,

when I look at this feast," I said laughing, but added quickly, as I remembered the absent husband, "It wasn't for George, was it?"

Mrs. Cranford laughed, "Same old Peter," she said. "Well, well – no, it wasn't for George. You needn't worry – but tell me…" Her attitude became serious. "How were you wounded? Can I help while you're away from the hospital? It's nothing bad, is it?"

I dismissed the subject as best I could by saying, "No, nothing much, they're pretty well healed now. A bullet wound in my arm, and some shrapnel in my side and leg. Side was the worst, but that's O.K. now. See? Nothing to worry about at all."

"But Peter –" began Mrs. Cranford. I was saved by a light knock on the hall door which heralded the entrance of Mrs. Taylor, who alleging she had heard the noise of reunion, wanted to tell Mrs. Cranford that if Peter wanted Tommy's room he could use it. She shook my hand, questioned me eagerly; and in my turn I enquired about Tommy, her son at sea with the Merchant Navy. Mrs. Cranford said I was here for a fortnight, and Mrs. Taylor excused herself retiring hurriedly, whether to contemplate the matter or to grieve over her rash offer, or merely to speed on some small domestic scheme, I can't say, but I was extremely grateful to her.

"I'll take your things up presently, Peter," said Mrs. Cranford.

"No, no," I hurriedly answered, "all I've got is contained in my respirator, as for those week-ends before I went away. Do you remember?"

"How can I forget? but you'll need more things, if you're stopping a fortnight, won't you?" she asked, or maybe advised.

"Well, I've sort of fixed that. Mother will be sending on some clothes for me, but they'll be going to the Blaydon. I'll warn Mrs. Dod about that, and ask her too if she could put Mother up for a week or so."

There was a pause, then repeating my thanks for the way

Friday

she had accepted my disconcerting arrival, I qualified my words by producing a ration card.

It was at this dramatic moment that footsteps sounded outside, footsteps approaching down the path. We ran together like children to the window. It was all dark. Suddenly realising that it was after black-out time, we scurried round putting up pieces of paper, pulling curtains, and generally concealing all lights from view outside – less from the Boche than P. C. Stott, the local Constable. The sound of the steps was by the door as we completed the rushed operations – was it George or the Constable? The outer door opened; it must be George. The hall door opened, and I gasped incredulously as the great man advanced into the room. He did not see me, and his first words were, "I say, Dore, that black-out should have been up much earlier."

But Dora Cranford knew her George, "I know George, but I forgot. Look who's here."

George looked, perceived me, and as though he'd seen me only last week-end, shook my hand, saying, "By Jove, you're looking fit, Peter man. I'm pleased to see you, man. But I could do with some food, eh, Dora?"

I noticed how he still used the name Dore when he was grieved with her, and Dora when he was pleased. He turned to me again, "What say you, Peter, eh? Have you brought your ration card with you, man?"

I grinned sheepishly, and answered, "It's great of you to have me to stay," and then, "I'm awfully pleased to see you again. Are you keeping well? I mean, shall we be able to have a drink together to-night?"

George looked at me quizzically, and having read ill into my innocent request, said, "Hah! You're a bad lad. Yes, I'm keeping pretty fit. But, excuse me, while I hang my coat in the hall," and aside for my special benefit, "And perform my ablutions, what?"

The Letters

I laughed – George's outlook on life was both stern and humorous, so that he won the hearts of all upon whom he bestowed the benevolence of his personality; there was wit in his most obvious remark, but whether that wit was always intentional I am not at liberty to say, sufficient that his light-hearted joviality and good will made him the main-stay of many a convivial party. George and I had much more in common at this meeting than previously, for I too had now experienced what he called "the holocaust of Armageddon", or at least, a small portion of it (which seemed to me a very large portion at the time).

"Peter, I've just poured you out another cup of tea." It was Mrs. Cranford's voice from inside the room. I called, "Thank you," as I saw her disappearing into the tiny kitchenette.

I sat down to contemplate it all again. The whole room was glimmering warmly, the orange-coloured wallpaper, the orange shaded lamps, and the scarlet embers of the coals all contributing towards the sheltering, protective atmosphere which hung low in the room; happiness clung to those flickering shadows; memories filled the room that night in wispy festoons, which I conjured out of yesterday.

Suddenly I remembered Mrs. Cranford was working outside, so making a hurried choice of the records we had loved before, I put them onto the playing rack, switched out the lamp, and lifted the latch of the outer door to walk from a dream into a rattling reality. There was Mrs. Cranford prettily clad in a blue and yellow flowered apron, which attracted my immediate attention and remark. My presence slowed the washing and drying process, though Mrs. Cranford said how much quicker the work was being done; but she had to humour me lest I should desperately volunteer for a mass of duties in which I could only prove a disastrous handicap to all concerned for two whole weeks.

What uneducated yet accurate students in the science of psychology are women! Can there be anything to this feminine intuition business? I felt the subject warranted meditation.

Friday

When we had finished we went back into the sitting room. Here the magic of light had interchanged with the magic of sounds: the gramophone brought the old memories tumbling vividly before my mind, as each melody, each orchestration pursued one another swiftly. George had dissolved the visual atmosphere by putting on the main light. He could never understand, he said, how we ever tolerated the half-light given by that orange lamp. (He understood very well, but a man of his quality must keep the dignified appearance of serene though bending superiority.)

With conversation, the serving and eating of supper, the time passed swiftly by, so that it was nearly nine o'clock before the three of us emerged from number five. George and I arranged to meet Mrs. Cranford at the "Cottage" after closing time.

The air was chilly, fresh, a fact which George discovered almost immediately.

"Wrap yourselves well," he instructed.

Obediently Mrs. Cranford and I closed our coat collars nearer to our throats, hunched our shoulders, increased our pace. I found myself amazed at the astonishing sagacity of the great gentleman, who so kindly made felt his wisdom and will.

The moon was rising, as we walked through the empty main street past the cold store buildings. The water of the Tyne was high, but not swollen or hurried; the moonbeams reflected eerily upon still deep patches further up the river, where thick dark trees clustered down to the edge of the far bank.

Just as we were crossing the bridge, we heard the piercing laugh of a girl. Automatically turning our heads towards the Post Office, whence the sound came, we saw what appeared to be a man in uniform escorting a female along the road to Brandon Mill.

George muttered, "That Griefly girl, I expect."

Dora said, "The air smells so sweet to-night."

The Letters

I smiled.

Mrs. Cranford left us at the other end of the bridge, tapping happily away from us, vigorously swinging her right arm to maintain equilibrium and keeping herself warm at the same time; for it was a very cold night, as George repeated when we entered the thick warmth of the Ship lounge.

The room was only half full. A merry fire crackled in the grate. Two amber lights in chained bowls of that colour illuminated the futuristic wall paper; this was quite new to me. When I mentioned the change, George told me that the owner of the pub, some artless bourgeois, had compelled the proprietress, Mrs. Black, to have it pasted up.

As we seated ourselves at a table near the fire, I glanced round to see if there was anybody present whom I knew, but there was not. One half of the circle about the fire was occupied by a chattering group of the local Tank unit's officers, who eyed me suspiciously, but smiled frankly to George: the other half was used by ourselves, and some miscellaneous entities engaged in deep conversation: outside this circle few braved, but there was a thin, pale youth dressed in bright tweeds, and wearing suede shoes – his eyes bleared, as he sopped up his glittering ale. He sat in a corner near a small man with a large stomach, a nose which twitched, a moustache which bristled; this little man leaned over a map, making copious notes between sips of whiskey.

"Good evening, Jane," I heard George say. Looking up, I saw the maid who had been with Mrs. Black two years ago.

"Great Heavens, Jane, how are you? You've not changed a bit. I never expected to see you here still! How's everything?" I asked.

Jane was startled: failed to recognise me; then wrongly identifying me as a Mr. Webb of an intervening regiment, finally said, "Oh yes! the Buffs!" – in a tone, which conveyed to the gentlemen of the Tank unit that here was indeed an officer from a

Friday

really worth-while regiment. The gentlemen of the Tank unit renewed their halted chatter.

"Oh yes," continued Jane innocently, "We've missed you boys. Never had any to match them since the Rifle Brigade. They were nice. Well, I was surprised and couldn't for the life of me think who you were, sir. I am glad you're back. What can I get for you, sir?" – then perceiving Mr. Cranford's amused face beaming blandly, she added, as though this was a moment for general reckoning, "You look better now, sir? Are you keeping fit?"

"Not so bad, Jane, not so bad," said the great man, "but I'll be a lot better if you bring me two beers, eh?"

Jane, looking at me again astonished, departed, her eyes unseeing, her ears closed, so that requests for more drinks from a Major of the local Tank unit were ignored. I watched the furious Major rise to his feet, stride over to the bell by the door, press the bell furiously, and return to his chair. Mrs Black entered answering the bell's summons. George called to her.

"I've brought someone to see you Mrs. Black."

Greetings, reminiscences, Jane's interruption with the beer, a short argument between George and I as to who should pay for it, an au-revoir to Mrs. Black and the Major, was at last served.

George and I quietly drank our beer, discussed this war and the last from a soldier's view-point, ordered more beer, and fell into a short silence of thought, interrupted by the clinking of mugs, the continuous opening and shutting of the bar door, and the hubbub of talk.

A young man and a girl entered. They sat down in the corner opposite the thin young man; they appeared to be dreaming.

"There's more than one way of looking at it –" "You can't say that, you don't know what they do." "Naf! the police! What do –"

The Letters

I had been listening dreamily to fragments of conversation from the group next to the fire on our right; at the mention of the word "police", for some reason, I found myself at once intensely interested. Thinking it over afterwards, I remembered Mr. Bromley's parting words to me earlier in the evening; the unconscious association of ideas was the reason.

Looking slowly round towards the group, I saw three old men. One was a most inspiring figure with the portly frame of a Greek merchant, the scarlet face of an English brewer, and a long white moustache, which could only have been grown by a man of the Victorian era; he appeared to be the Oracle of the other two, who referred to him periodically on higher questions, or asked for his opinion on certain points. The others had spoken the words, which had attracted my attention; one of them was a hard, little man with a lined, tanned face, a pointed nose, and head like a small cannon ball; the other was taller than his partner, though just as gaunt, his chin a dark blue, his hair long, black, his eyes sparkling with the passion of his feelings, so freely expressed. The former was speaking now. I looked away and listened, as he addressed the man with the cannon-ball head.

"– and there's certain things which don't come out in the papers, isn't that so, Mr. James?" (This question obviously directed to the portly Victorian) I imagined Mr. James nodded his assent, for the gaunt man's voice continued: "What was he doing out there at that time of night, eh? That's what I want to know. What was he doing out there?"

The higher-pitched voice of the other man answered, "He might have gone for a walk, and got hit. It was dark."

"Silly, a tank makes enough noise, don't it?" said the gaunt man with crushing scorn.

"Yes, but he might have climbed the bank out of the way, him seeing it was dark, and then fell at the last moment."

"Very likely, very likely!" sneered the gaunt man.

Friday

"Well, I can't see you've anything to be suspicious about. You've all gone daft over this, you have. Keep on talking about murder, and suicide, just because of an accident."

"What about what our Will heard Charlie Stott say?" countered the gaunt man triumphantly.

I listened eagerly, for I began to understand a little more than I did when I first met Mr. Bromley hours before; but I was still puzzled. The name "Stott" was significant, for he was the village's unpopular, local Constable.

"Yes, but that Charlie would say anything to make himself look big."

How true, I thought.

"Yes," agreed the gaunt man staunchly, "but Will wasn't supposed to have heard what he did, you know. That's what I mean. It's queer. What do you say, Mr. James?"

Before I could hear Mr. James' valuable opinion, George interrupted.
"Are you tired, Peter man? Are you feeling well?"

"Yes, I'm fine. Sorry. I was just thinking," I replied apologetically.

"By Jove it's good to make the old times again. Let's have some more quaff," he said, beckoning jovially to Jane. The order made, I asked George if anything amiss had happened in Halt Bridge recently. This question obviously surprised him; he tried to conceal this by a mysterious silence. For a long time, he did not reply, but leaning back in his chair, and placing the tips of his fingers together, he looked at me through half-closed eyes; I had seen him assure this attitude before, so I knew that he was considering profoundly.

"Yes, Peter." Pause. "How came you by this knowledge?"

The Letters

I explained how I had met Mr. Bromley in the train, and what he had said to me. George answered, "That man Bromley's a fool. He talks above himself. But there is some queer talk amongst the proletariat of the village, and you know how scandal – and rumour – spread in Halt Bridge."

I nodded my agreement. He continued again with the same grave voice, slow impressive phrases, the clear composed English; his chin forced forward as he concluded any fighting sentence, his eyes opening widely as he introduced any startling information – such was the mood of George Cranford.

"And – Peter – as close to the village as Sidley Bridge –" he paused. I had detected contempt in the way he had said "Sidley Bridge", so I waited impatiently for his next words.

"As near as that – a man –" here his eyebrows raised and his hand tapped the table edge sharply, so sharply that a large portion of both our beers was spilt "has been killed." He laughed bitterly.

I daringly commented, "The war on their door-steps, as it were."

"Ah," cried George admiringly, "I see you have insight. Yes, around this dead man – a man, mark you, who was visiting Halt Bridge – visiting – er, rumour has it – that Griefly girl." (I knew Jane Griefly when she had shocked the Buffs by her indiscriminate heart-breaking of two officers, three sergeants, and a lance corporal.)

George coughed, "The man was a naval chap – poor fellow – run over by a tank but – rumour – mind – it is only rumour – has it that he committed suicide – due to love – or disappointment in love – they conceive cunningly, and how cunning they can be! – they recall accurate details in their rumours! They report actual words spoken! They know all about –"

To return George to the main point of his story, away from his theories and relevant anecdotes, I maliciously swallowed the

Friday

beer left in my mug, then as politely as possible said, "Excuse me one moment, but the hour advances! Will you have another?"

George said he would, so I called to Mrs. Black who was disappearing through the door. George had been disturbed. Like all great men disturbed he found difficulty recalling where his oration had been interrupted, so I helpfully asked, as I paid for the beer brought by Jane, "And what really did happen to this unfortunate sailor?"

"Some say he was murdered," was the quick reply.

"What! really?" I exclaimed. "You don't mean Sidley's had a real murder? Impossible! Say, that's exciting. But what's the uncertainty? How was he killed? Why aren't you sure about it? I mean, what's all the mystery about? Everybody seems to be talking about it. Why? When did it happen?"

George was quite confused by this unjust, muddled barrage of questions.

"Eh, man," he said testily. "Give me a chance. One thing at a time."

I apologised; and George said boyishly, "You're impetuous. And at your age, I suppose I –" He went into the vast details of his youth, which I had heard so many times in the past as to be able to repeat them myself. I pretended to look attentive, at the same time trying to listen to the medley of words issuing from the two gossiping old men, still presided over by Mr. James, who was grunting. I strained my ears to cipher the grunts, husky grunts, which formed the following word sequence:

"Murder – unck – yes – murderunk – Will's-trusty – believe-him – heard Stott he says – unk – heard him talking to – Inspector-bloke – told him what the doctor said –" Heavy breathing was the reason for a short pause here, then the gulping sound of large quantities of gurgling alcohol before he proceeded.

The Letters

"Said the corpse was dead before – the time the tanks – unk – unk – passed."

"Yes," the gaunt man hoarsely added as if to conclude the matter.

I no longer listened to their voices, no longer heard the publican murmurings; I could only think – a murder! here! Why should not George and I investigate this? why not? What fun it would be! I pictured myself as Watson to the logical will of a Sherlock Cranford.

Seeing that George was drinking, I gathered he had completed his famous autobiography. I quickly said, "About this Sidley mystery – what about investigating? Sort of privately? Wouldn't that be fun?"

George thought it would not. Disappointed, I said, "But we might get somewhere, and it might prove quite exciting."

George laughed, "So you want to set up as a private detective, as soon as you land? Wild dreams, Peter boy! You want to be a Javert, eh? The ruthless police officer – aha!"

George seized his hat quite viciously, and put it on. As I imitated him, Mrs. Black cooed 'Time' from the half-open doorway and one of the lights went out.

"Well timed," I said.

"I should know the ins and outs of this place by now," admitted George, picking up his stick. All about us was a general scraping of chairs, a shuffling, a rustle of clothes; mugs made their miserable last clatter; and farewells sounded on all sides mingling with goodnights.

Before we left, we called out good wishes to the ladies in charge. The night air as we stepped outside was icy, but refreshing, reviving, wakening.

Friday

"My word," said George with feeling, "this air's got some pep, what? Pah! – delightful."

I agreed, but my thoughts were on the lines of Whimsey, Poirot, or even Dr. Thorndyke.

"Now, now my young Javert, what thoughts have you? Are you thinking of Jean Valjean? Eh? Javert!" George said the last name with a snarl expressive of the omnipotence of the Law. I laughed.

"You just see," I said; and George chuckled.

The "Cottage" was a one-room, one-storey house, situated on the river's edge behind the Blaydon. Thither we repaired for a further reunion with the Thompsons, heart-friends of the Cranfords, and likewise evacuated from Newcastle.

When I got to bed that night, I was drunk – not with the quantity of beer consumed, but with excess of happiness in being amongst sincere, and loved friends once again. I could not get to sleep, but lay thinking over the events of the day for a long time. Could this really be true? I was almost afraid to sleep. Instead of the Cranfords and the Thompsons, might I not waken to the Libyan scrub, or to the tossing of the Hospital ship? Still pondering, I dozed off into a Fairyland of happy dreams.

CHAPTER II: MURDER - SATURDAY

The next morning I wakened to the thunder of guns. I thought I was in the desert again, until my mind became orientated and I realised that the milk-train had just tumbled past my window on its way to Newcastle. I turned over, yawned, and fell asleep almost at once. When I woke up again, I opened my eyes to see three things, the first was a cup of tea, the second was Mrs. Cranford, and the third was a ray of Winter sun-shine lighting the foot of my bed. "Good Heavens!" I cried sitting up in bed with a start. "What's the time? is it late? I'm awfully sorry, Mrs. Cranford, but I must have overslept. You see —"

"Oh! Peter when shall we cure you?" Dora interrupted. "It's not late, and you can stay in bed just as long as you like. You're here for a rest and a holiday. I've brought you some tea."

"Thanks very much," I said, "That's grand. Can I help with the breakfast, or anything?"

"No, there's nothing to do. You lie down, and go to sleep again. George isn't up yet."

I smiled, "Well that's the ideal time to step in on the bath-room situation, or should I make sure and let George go in first?"

Mrs. Cranford laughed, and tripped out of the door-way; as I sipped the hot sweet tea, I listened dreamily to her footsteps tapping down the stairs. Presently I jumped out of bed, crept warily to the door, and onto the landing, armed with the toilet equipment from my haversack. All was quiet. I silently advanced to the head of the stairs, slowly picking up my feet so as not to let George know of my intention. I clasped the banister resolutely. I took my first step downwards, and thought 'nothing to fear now, he must still be asleep.' Suddenly, my blood felt icy. My eyes reflected horror, for at the moment of apparent triumph, I heard a voice say, "Aha! what is

Saturday

this? what is this I see? my young Javert! uh? Javert up stalking so early? Y'know you should make less noise, Peter man – as a detective!" It was George.

Breakfast was completed with a discussion on our programme for the day: George declared that he was going for a walk, and I agreed to accompany him.

Dora said she had a lot of work to do, though what there was to do in that one room which could keep her occupied for a whole morning I did not understand; but I politely refrained from comment. I asked George if he minded calling in at the Blaydon for a few minutes, as I wanted to see Mrs. Dod about a number of arrangements; George said he thought that was an admirable scheme, as long as we saw Mrs. Dod at an hour suitable for the purchase of stimulants, a point which I thought he unduly stressed. However, we eventually stopped talking for a period sufficient to get ourselves clad ready for the proposed walk, by which time it was just after ten o'clock. We bade Dora farewell, and stepped into the icy tang of a chill, delightful air – a cold English morning. I breathed deeply. This was really England.

He walked quickly up the lane to the cross-roads and the crossing, where the two gates were closed. As we waited George told me all about these gates, which were fated always to close, or be about to be closed, whenever he approached. I listened with a close attention due to the great man's pearly words, cast as they were before swing my hog's ears; and all the while I gazed at the frost-covered slopes of the two ranges running unevenly, parallel to the Tyne; it was a beautiful sight. George stamped his feet because he was impatient to continue the walk; I stamped my feet, because they were colder than they had been for two years. Eventually a train, chuffing and squeaking, clanged by; the gates opened, and we were off, George setting a ranting pace, his eyes streaming with the cold, his nose beacon-red, and his stick swinging dexterously.

The street seemed unusually full of people. Outside the

The Letters

Leather-shop, I could see a small crowd chattering, gesticulating. Occasionally a body would peel away to be replaced by another almost at once. Some folks talking beyond my ken sailed past us unseeing, only avoiding certain collision with us because we hurriedly parted out of their way. George must have noticed the bustle, and gathered that there was something "in the air", for he said jovially, "Eh, my Javert – what is this? Do you see what I see?"

I answered with a rude, "Umm."

"I saw no news of any importance in the paper this morning, did you?" asked George.

I confessed to not having read the paper, feeling that I had dropped fifty per cent in his estimation. We passed the crowd, from which drifted such remarks as "this morning", "Sidley", "that sailor". I noticed the attraction appeared to be a wild-eyed youth, a labourer, who was talking and waving his arms.

"I say you know, I think something's up – locally," I remarked, adding suddenly, as a thought came to my mind, "Do you think it's anything to do with this murder business? I mean –"

George interrupted with, "What's that man?" he laughed. "You're letting your imagination – get the better of you. My Javert! It's probably a new bit of war rumour," and adding enlighteningly, "or something."

"Yes," I said and looked at George, but his thoughts were far away.

We were about to go from the pavement to the bridge when I saw Mr. Thompson coming across. Even as I mentioned this two motor-cycles ridden at a noisy pace screamed towards us over the bridge, swerved violently round the bend, and at a high speed disappeared up the Haltwhistle road; they were policemen. A moment later a police car skidded round the corner, changed gear, vanishing recklessly after the speed-cops. In my mind the words "Sidley", "that sailor", "this morning", which I had heard from the

Saturday

crowd, churned over, making a fantastic connection with the police racing at that hour of the morning in the direction of Sidley. Where did "that sailor" come in to it? "That sailor" – who was he?

We reached the bridge as Mr. Thompson crossed.

"Good morning, Bart," greeted George.

Bart Thompson was in a great state of excitement. Ignoring our salutations, he said, "Have you heard? My family are talking all about it. Seems there was trouble last night. Queer thing, can't make it out."

"What's all this? What's it all about? Come Bart, explain yourself," said George with mingled curiosity and indignation.

Bart was pleased to find us ignorant of his novel information; so secreting himself wisely into a nook in the parapet of the bridge, he puffed at his pipe, whilst George and I, trying not to appear too eager, leaned carefully against the wall, and looked into the river. Bart came to the point with such surprising suddenness that we both exclaimed, "What!"

"There was murder in the village last night," he said.

"What!" I repeated.

"By Jove!" said George.

"True," said Bart.

George looked sideways at me as though as to say, 'Eh Peter man, you know something about this – what have you been doing?' but I think the idea behind the look was 'Eh Peter! You win. I like this. We'll investigate, man,' or was that just conceit?

Anyway, we learnt that Bart had very little data other than that somebody had been murdered, somewhere near Halt Bridge, sometime last night; so, bidding him a short adieu, we arranged to

The Letters

meet him in the "Ship" before lunch.

When we reached the Blaydon Hotel, I said to George, "Come on in with me. Mrs Dod's the local Encyclopaedia, she's bound to know something about all this." She did not let me down; George and I sat enthralled at her lurid account.

"Ooh – I am glad to see you both. Come in. The place is in a dreadful state. Have you heard about it?" she exclaimed in one breath. We smiled.

"Bonny lad," she said – referring to me, thought George; and to me, thought I.

"Mrs. Dod," George began pompously, "I have been given to understand –"

"The murder," supplemented Mrs Dod. "Have you heard?"

We shook our heads.

"You want to know all about it?" she guessed.

I nodded. She became almost serious, as she said, "It's young Jane Griefly. Last night she was seen going for a walk with a naval officer from Jackson's. They were going out towards Brandon Hill, as it was getting dark."

"That's it!" George cried. "Peter, we've got something. That's interesting! By Jove man, we saw the start of it! Don't you remember the laughter which attracted our attention as we were crossing the bridge last night?"

I recalled it vividly, and now the word "sailor" was clear to me too. We were in the thick of the mystery. I set myself to make George more interested than he obviously was.

"Yes, Mrs Dod?" I said.

"My bairn!" she answered with a laugh; and George looked

Saturday

at me sideways again.

She continued, "Well – as far as I know, though I don't know very much – it's only what I've heard, but as far as I know –"

"Yes, yes," said George impatiently. Mrs. Dod laughed again, and her personality elated us both.

"Not so fast! – Well, as I was saying," she went on, "they walked as far as Sidley Bridge, and that's where it happened. He must have pushed her off the top – and you know how high it is!"

George nodded his head. In the centre the bridge at Sidley was at least thirty or forty feet high.

"And what was the motive?" I enquired.

George began to say his piece about Javert, when Mrs. Dod, undaunted, replied, "They don't know that yet, but the Officer left Jackson's early this morning and caught the first train into Newcastle. He must have done it. The police are looking for him."

"When was the body discovered, and by whom?" I asked. I noticed that George no longer made his mocking observations; there was a strange glint in his eyes, as he keenly awaited the answer to my question.

"Funny boys," said Mrs. Dod with a pretty smile. "I'm not the police. What do you think I know?"

How contradictory! How like a woman! How like Mrs. Dod! I thought, but I said with an encouraging smile, "Well?"

"Well, if you must know," she said with artificial reluctance, "the body was found some way down from the bridge, where the river had carried it. Isn't it horrible talking about it? Anyway, a farmer's boy saw it there. He was leaning on the parapet, waiting for his 'bus."

Suddenly she looked at the clock, "My goodness," she

The Letters

exclaimed. "A quarter to eleven! I'll never get done."

However – before we left, I made my arrangements with her for putting up my mother for a week or so; she said she "would be thrilled": I also asked if she'd mind receiving any of my mail, which she said she'd "be delighted to do".

We left the Blaydon to walk slowly up the road to the Castle, both of us silent, deep in thought. We turned back; had coffee at the Cottage; met Bart at the Ship; and returned in time for lunch with Dora at one o'clock.

"What a very pleasant way to spend a morning," I remarked.

"Yes," said George with peculiar emphasis, then, "Dora, have you heard about the Griefly girl?"

It appeared that Dora was in full possession of all the facts – that she had not asked for them, we must understand, but that she had in the course of her work encountered Mrs. Taylor, who had told her all about it. "Ee, what a dreadful thing," she concluded.

It was while we were having our lunch that George made his startling announcement. He had just finished eating his first course, when clasping his hands together, and resting his arms on the table, he said, "Dora! – Peter!" slowly, dramatically looking from Mrs. Cranford to myself, and back again.

"Dora! You are listening, Dora, are you not?"

"Yes, George, of course, but Peter must have his sweet."

I wished Mrs. Cranford would not say things like that; her words brought a terrifying glance from George, so that I felt smaller than half a piastre.

"Dora, never mind. I am speaking."

Silence ensued. Dora and I stared at George. His stage now set, he spoke: "I find there is a lull in my business affairs. The war

Saturday

makes – changes. The war –"

"Oh come on, George," interrupted Dora, "the pudding's getting cold."

George looked very injured, but his eyes burned with wild fire.

"Since I may not have another – chance like this – for a holiday –"

"George! …" cried Dora, "That will be lovely, won't it Peter?"

I was about to answer, when George said, "Wait – I have not said all. I must confess – I have been influenced in my decision – by local events."

I looked up amazed; George noticed this, for he said, "Yes, Peter I have been thinking – I have an idea, an idea, which came to me – this morning, Peter man! together – you and I – we'll track down the murderer."

Dora suppressed a laugh, and went into the kitchenette to get the next course. I wanted to help her, but George grasped my wrist.

"We must not let an innocent man be condemned."

I replied instantly, "Then you are thinking what I have thought? We're agreed. Say, that's great. When do we start? That naval officer's absolutely innocent. You know, I think these two tragedies are connected. Remember? The other man was a sailor, and he too associated with Jane Grifbey, or Grisley, or whatever her name is."

"Griefly," said George briefly.

"Well, Peter what are you thinking?"

"Just this," I said enthusiastically, "Isn't it possible that these two naval men were related? Isn't it then simple for an outside person to influence the course of these two men to gain his, or her own end – in some way?"

"Romance, Peter man, romance," said George.

That afternoon George went to visit a friend of his at Brandon Mill, while Mrs. Cranford and I had tea with Bart, Jean and Beryl at the Cottage. Beryl and I had a lot to tell each other, a lot to say; in the early evening we decided to go to the local Cinema to see Jack somebody in some murder film, which we enjoyed. I escorted her afterwards to the Ship, where we had arranged to meet the others.

"I feel like Jack Thing-a-me-bob. George and I are going to solve the Sidley mysteries," I said.

Beryl was intrigued. She's a charming girl. I asked her to join our investigations, which would probably start to-morrow. She thought it a great idea, but tomorrow she was going out with Capt. Ebbse of the Tank regiment, and the next day she was at work again with the A.R.P. at Hentham. I said she must be our "Hentham, and local Army, Detective agent", and she smilingly agreed.

Inside the Ship we were greeted by the family: Bart drew up two more chairs, George ringing the bell ordered drinks, and the ladies twittered. The lounge was more full to-night than on the previous evening, and the army was conspicuously present. A tall dark man with a black moustache, and a dashing smile hailed Sybil, was invited to the table, and introduced to me as Capt. Ebbse; he was the type of man who promptly began talking about the army, a subject to which I have a particular aversion. I could see George had been speaking before our arrival for there was a sad, baffled expression on his face, as he sipped his ale. Rudely ignoring a question of the Captain about Italian grenades, or something equally abortive, I asked George if there was any news.

"News Peter, news," a happy glow reflected from ale came into his eyes, "I have real news." He looked at Capt. Ebbse, then

Saturday

pointing to me said, "This is my Javert. We are out to kill," and as he said this, he banged his mug on the table.

"Careful, George," said Dora.

George ignored the remark, saying, "I have news for you – Peter. Indeed, as I was saying – ah – to the others just now." Pause. "The naval officer – er – has been – arrested." He paused again for effect. "His name is Lieutenant Cummings of the Merchant Navy. And this is the point – the man killed by the tank the other day – that sailor – that unhappy man – was his – brother!" There was triumph in his eyes as he said the word "brother". "He was arrested this afternoon while lunching at the 'Turks Head'"

"Well, well," I said, "that's that. We can get moving now. These darned, bungling police. Typical! P.C. Stott will have something to do with this. Though," I added leniently, "it does look black on the Lootenant."

"Yes, but we shall prove them wrong Peter – eh? Won't we?" asked George with a sinister nod.

Capt. Ebbse lifted an enquiring eyebrow, and spoke out of the right-hand corner of his mouth with a superior, mocking affectation, "My word, Mr. Cranford – you're up to something then?"

George ignored him, ignored everybody, and said, "And there's another thing, the most important development so far – food for hours of thought. The doctor's autopsy!"

"Now George!" cautioned Dora

But George said, "Jane Griefly was pregnant."

"George!" said Jean.

"I say," said Capt. Ebbse.

"Really? Well, well," said I.

The Letters

Food for thought indeed, as George had said. If Jane Griefly was pregnant at the time of her death, then who had been the cause? Who had killed her? why had she been killed, or had she committed suicide? or had it been an accident?

Cummings certainly had not killed the girl, because his every action was so absurdly obvious. The police solution was that Cummings had come down to Halt Bridge intending to see Jane; had proved attractive to her in his officer's uniform; had enticed her to Sidley, an ideal place for murder; and had killed the girl: that night there were no other trains to Newcastle, so Cummings had caught the first on the following day; the pregnancy, they alleged had probably been caused by the younger brother, a reason for his suicide, which the perverse mind of Cummings was avenging; at the 'Turks Head' hotel, he had imagined himself safe, for nobody was aware of his identity in Halt Bridge, not even Mr. Jackson at the "Dutch House". How childish; how unlikely; how lacking in human understanding! It was a textbook answer evolved from routine enquiries, and automaton minds – possibly efficient, but so 'narrow'.

That night I lay in bed thinking over the whole situation, wondering, questioning, but to no avail. If Cummings had not killed Jane, then who had? How was it he went out with the girl, and returned without her? Why should the police wickedly assume Cummings' brother responsible for the girl's pregnancy? What was the connection, if any, between the two deaths? Were they both accidents? Were they both suicides? Were they both murders? Was the same individual the perpetrator of both? What exactly had happened?

At last sleep overwhelmed my hazy thoughts.

CHAPTER III: GEORGE INVESTIGATES - SUNDAY

To Mrs. Cranford's astonishment, George and I were up early on Sunday morning. We were out of Halt Bridge walking down the Haltwhistle road before half past nine. The morning was icy cold. We both wore gloves, and I felt nervous with a civilian muffler about my neck, a muffler which contrasted conspicuously with my khaki attire. However, nobody who was concerned would see it in this part of the country, as George pointed out.

As we walked, our breath made little clouds before us; a Winter sun struggled to light the frosted ground and trees with golden streaks; the Tyne waters gurgled softly, incessantly on our left; a tractor wheezed mechanically somewhere out of view on our right, and an occasional army truck, civilian car, or lorry rushed past us with noisy hooter blare, which made George very angry.

George broke the silence prevailing between us. "A beautiful morning – to be out so early. How sad it is – that we do not enjoy this pleasure of nature more often," he said with great fervour.

"It's grand," I said.

"'Grand', Peter, 'grand'," repeated George, horrified at my inadequate description of the day, and painting it in glowing terms as follows: "Why man, it's beautiful, beautiful, what do you say? Don't you think – it's beautiful?"

I assured him that I did, and we walked on in silence again.

Soon we reached a turning off the main road, which led downhill over a bridge, turned to the left, and wound its way along to Sidley Hall: the bridge crossing the river at this point was known as Sidley Bridge. We had reached the first step in our investigations. I was excited.

The Letters

We looked down into the running waters, and leaned on the parapet of the bridge. I shuddered; it seemed a tremendous fall. I gazed round at the fields, the woods. How desolate the spot was! At night, how quiet and peaceful – only the bubbling Tyne! What an ideal place to commit murder! George was thinking the same; he said, "Whoever did this could not have thought of a better place. We're up against brains, Peter. We've got a job, a job, oh man!"

"Let's go down and see if the police have missed anything during their search," I suggested.

"You lead the way, Peter. I'm not so young – not so young as I was."

We walked back to a part of the wall suitable for climbing. I clambered down onto the steep, grassy slope, and helped the complaining George as he pulled himself up after me. Carefully we walked and slithered down the bank to the wide pathway by the water's edge. We both parted here, stealthily advancing this way and that with lifted knees and heads bowed staring on the ground. George poked and stabbed indiscriminately with his walking stick – like Mr. Pickwick, I thought. I glanced about eagerly but in vain; and I was just getting bored when I heard a shout from under the bridge. "Peter, man, Peter. Come here, man."

I ran back up the path till I was beside George. Breathless, I asked what he had found.

"Look, man," said George impressively pointing with his stick into the dark, swirling waters. I looked, saw nothing, and said so.

"What's that, Peter? Can't see?" said George gaily, "Why, look there. D'you see that light-coloured rock there by two large black ones?" As he spoke, he wagged his stick in the water. "Have it up, man. Let's see."

The river varied between a few inches, and a few feet in depth in this area, so that I had no difficulty raising the rock. George

Sunday

knelt beside me on his knees as I landed the stone.

"Look at them! Long, black hairs! They're smeared on hard with flesh and water-slime – that's what's held them. Do you see, man? Somebody has used this as a weapon. Whoever used it, struck a pretty vicious blow by the way these hairs have stuck – my word!"

"Black hair!" I muttered, "Jane Griefly had ginger hair, didn't she?" Then enthusiastically, "Well done, George. First victory to you, Mr. Holmes. Terrific!" and I patted him on the back.

He laughed. "By Jove, Peter, we're getting somewhere."

"Since that's black hair, it's not Jane Griefly's, and the only other person who's been hit around here was young Cummings. Now Cummings had an accident upon the road up there. Suppose he had been killed by somebody down here – let's say X – then dragged up that slope and dropped through the hedge under a passing car? In this case you see X was fortunate enough to find a tank which nearly covered all his tracks by completely squashing the poor chap. Suppose – then doesn't that mean something?"

I paused, looking to George for encouragement. He stood there with arms folded, his old trilby hat on the back of his head, his feet astride, a small man with an elegantly curved nose, bright intelligent eyes, a keen strong mouth, a veritable Napoleon I thought.

"Peter," he spoke slowly, "We are on the brink – of danger. We are pitting our lives – against brains. We – must be wary."

I smiled, "That's fine. Let's get on with this search. Now look, if I'm right the man we're looking for must be very strong and fit. Look at that slope. It's enormous! He must have first killed the sailor, dragged him up there and along the hedge-row to a suitable place." My words jumbled out inconsistently: "Why! if we look we may find the hole in the hedge, or something of their clothes torn on the way up. You can't drag a bloke all that way without doing some damage

The Letters

to your clothes. Let's see. We've got this taped".

"Steady, man! Steady," said George sternly. "Yes, you are right – we must search that bank. But I must say, Peter, I don't like the idea of climbing up it again."

I laughed, and we began the laborious climb. We were half way up when George exclaimed, "Peter, man," and I regretted having climbed so far ahead. I rejoined George almost sulkily. The man's eagle eyes, the Holmes in George, had made a further discovery – a small piece of tweed like a skag made in a coat. George put it in his pocket carefully saying, "This is a clue. If it comes from the sailor's jacket then it proves the sailor was probably murdered, unless by some chance he clambered up here and tore his coat. If it does not come from the sailor's jacket, then it probably comes from X's, unless some innocent person other than the sailor or X tore their coat here."

I nodded, and we rose to our feet. We were about to continue our climb, when we heard a loud laugh behind us. We both stood still, looked at each other, and turned slowly round. There on the bridge, leaning idly was an army officer, a full Lieutenant. "Good morning, Mr. Cranford," he said. "What a nice morning to play at Sexton Blake."

George was furious. "You – You – should learn – some manners," he stammered.

Then more calmly, "What – are you doing here, Mr. Edwards – er – may I ask?" I admired him.

Lieut. Edwards laughed smirkingly again. "I got the morning off. I'm a sick man. Thought I'd take a walk. And you, Mr. Blake? What are you doing? "

"Kindly keep your mannerless observations to yourself," I said catching hold of George's arm, as we stumbled up the bank together. We heard Mr. Edwards again laughing at us. At the top George puffed, "I wonder what he's doing here of all places? He's

Sunday

lazy, wouldn't walk out here for nothing."

"Who is he?" I asked.

"One of the local tank unit billeted on the Castle," George answered.

"Has he had anything to do with Jane Griefly at any time?"

"I'm not sure. We must enquire. But just now let's see about this hedgerow."

Feeling rebuked, I climber after him over a small wall; it separated the slope from a spinney of trees, which were sandwiched between the wall and the hedge, growing along the top of the road-bank. Walking parallel with the road we came after about fifty yards to a small gap – wide enough to allow the passage of a body; the gap had probably been made by children playing Indians.

"That's it," said George. "We've beaten the police. I tell you, Peter. Cummings' brother was murdered in cold blood."

We pushed our way through the gap, and began to walk back to the village.

"So far so good," George remarked, "but what we're forgetting is the most important thing of all. We're forgetting the motive. Why should anybody kill young Cummings? Why should –"

"Yes," I interrupted, "the girl – she was pregnant."

"Eh?" queried George. |

"Jane Griefly," I said. "Look, only a lover or a near relative of Jane's would want to kill Cummings as far as I can see, and then only if the person had reason to believe him to be the cause of her pregnancy."

"By Jove, Peter, you've got something there, man. A lover

or a – near relative! Her father perhaps? – or a lover?" And he smiled, "Edwards?"

We laughed. "I wonder," I said.

We were warm after our long walk and exertions. The sun was high, pale, stately. I carried my gloves and muffler. As we entered Halt Bridge we again seemed to meet a thick cloud of mystery, and a sensation of tenseness; passing the Post Office we saw people hurrying along the street towards the station; and coming round the corner, we saw a large crowd being organised by P.C. Stott at the entrance to the Church.

"What's happened now?" said George.

We looked at each other quickly, and stalked down the street with great fervour. An ambulance turned the corner from the road by the railway into the main-street; it stopped outside the Church just as we reached the edge of the crowd.

"What's all this?" George asked one of the crowd, an elderly farmer.

The man was willing to tell all he knew. "It's old Mr. Griefly – done hisself in. Must have been upset over his girl. Threw hisself off the Church tower, he did."

"Thank you," said George, and added quietly to me, "Have a look at his coat. Quick!"

I had to move fast for the ambulance men with sheet and stretcher were already pushing through the crowd to the corpse. The Vicar I noticed standing on his Church-steps, a depressed expression on his face – he must have thought, "If only they would flock to me like this every Sunday."

I went round to the side of the Church wall, climbed over, and walked across to where the body lay, keeping behind Stott's back. Mr. Griefly was a mess, but war was messy, and I had seen

Sunday

it before. I looked at the coat.

"Hi! you –! What do you think you're up to?" It was P.C. Stott, and the ambulance men.

"Sorry Officer," I said flatteringly, "I wanted to see if I knew the man. I was stationed here with the Buffs. You may remember me? I am staying with the Cranfords at No. 5 Rose Cottages. Please excuse me."

P.C. Stott glared angrily at me. Here was his chance to shine before the village, to put an officer in his place. "I've a good mind to hold you," he said, "but I'll let you off. You ought to know better. Now get out of here."

"Thank you, Constable," I replied facetiously. "Good morning. We shall be seeing each other again shortly – about some theories."

P.C. Stott was about to speak again, but I had rejoined George.

"Well done," said George. We were seated inside the "Station Hotel" and had ordered a pint apiece.

"It was easy," I said, "and – what's more – there was a small patch on his coat, a patch about the size of our skag discovery."

George was delighted. "That's one problem solved. But – my word Peter – who would ever have thought that an old chap like Griefly could commit a murder in cold blood! Poor old chap!"

"I'm not so sure," I said.

"Not so sure what?" asked George.

"Why, I'm not so sure that this little problem is solved."

Ernie Farmer, the barman, brought in two and a half pints. The half he consumed himself, beginning at the same time to give

The Letters

us a lurid account of the suicide.

A sound came to us from outside, a noise taken up by members of the bar next door. Somebody was shouting at the top of his voice over the general hubbub. We all three rushed to the window, kneeling on the seat to get a good view over the top of the Saloon Bar notice, which obscured the outer world. The crowd had almost dispersed, but a few remained still, and those who had left were dotted about like statues in the road, on the pavement, everywhere, all standing, staring up at the Church-tower. We stared up there too, but could see nothing. We listened to the voice as it bleated incessantly.

"There's a man up the tower – I saw him up there. He's still up there."

We could see the man who was shouting and so could P.C. Stott, for he came running back up the street as fast as his portly frame would allow. We rushed outside, leaving Ernie standing in his own door-way. P.C. Stott and the man who had shouted, pointed, and made such a noise, went inside the Church. We waited, this time at the head of the crowd, which was already gathering rapidly about us by the Church gates. After several minutes P.C. Stott and the noisy man emerged, escorting before them a tall, hefty individual; he it was whom we had seen up the tower.

"Good Heavens," George gasped.

"Great Scott!" I cried. "It's Mr. Ramon. What on earth has he got to do with all this?"

P.C. Stott pompously remarked to Mr. Ramon, as he approached:

"– And I'm holding you for the murder of Mr. Griefly."

The crowd heard Stott's words – as indeed they were supposed to do – and whistled in astonishment. P.C. Stott was walking on air.

Sunday

I was indignant. Before George could stop me, I had stepped forward saying, "That's not true. Mr. Griefly committed suicide, I'm sure of it."

P.C. Stott and prisoner stopped. All eyes turned on me. George saved the situation by saying to my amazement, "Good morning, Stott. This is my young friend. He's been injured – wounded you know, just returned from Libya."

The crowd was quite bewildered, and uttered sympathetic exclamations.

George added quickly, "You'll excuse us, won't you?"

"Why yes, sir, of course," replied P.C. Stott.

"What on earth – ?" I began to say.

"Sh! Peter, man. Come on back to the 'Station'. I'll tell you there."

"Look here, Peter man, we must work by ourselves until we can prove what we know. This evening we'll tell Stott our theories on the Cummings boy, but such an action as yours then – made on the impulse – can only cause trouble."

"But," I said, "Ramon's innocent. I've no idea what he was doing up in the tower, but it is so obvious –"

"Obvious to us with our new data – but not to him," said George wisely, waving his mug in the general direction of P.C. Stott. "They've nothing against Ramon; they can't detain him long – though he's got a lot of explaining to do. Never did like the man."

"Sorry," I said, "but what do you think about it all now? It seems to fit in. I'm speaking about the events as a whole and Mr. Griefly in particular. A man doesn't normally commit suicide on the death of his daughter, even if he is very fond of the child, even if it's an only child, even if the death is abnormal, does he?"

"It's a bit involved, but – No, I suppose he does not, but why should he kill himself, Peter? He might –"

I rather rudely interrupted with my answer to his last question, before George could embark on a description of our previous discussion.

"Excuse me, but isn't it possible Griefly killed himself for a number of strange reasons, which were pressing on his mind at the time? Let's – for instance – assume this: supposing Mr. Griefly was 'X'!"

"Yes," said George, "That's what I had thought."

"Well," I continued, "he must have had some proof – I don't know what, maybe we'll find out later – anyway, proof that a) his daughter was pregnant, and b) that Cummings was responsible. Here's an ample motive for murdering Cummings – if he was a particularly jealous, or loving, or proud father. Maybe he arranged, again I don't know how, to meet the boy at Sidley, I don't know why, and killed him, possibly in a fit of rage."

George remarked, "Griefly was an immensely strong man, one such as could have killed and dragged Cummings up that slope, and along to the gap."

"True," I agreed. "It all fits together. When he saw that he had taken a life in vain, for his daughter's death showed –"

"Just a minute, Peter – he must have thought himself partly to blame for his daughter's death as well! – since he had killed Cummings. You see, he'd only heard the police story of the boy's brother."

"That's right, we're doing fine. Why, the darned police are probably more responsible for the old chap's suicide than anything else. The point is that when he found he'd caused all this misery and death it must have played on his mind. He must as it were have found that nothing but evil comes of evil – however justifiable the

Sunday

cause. Voila!"

"Peter, man," George declared, "we 're a perfect partnership. It's time for lunch. Drink up your beer. We must go."

Dora was quite overwhelmed by all the news, and by our great wealth of theories. We talked all the way through lunch being still puzzled at the end, for we had really made little progress. What was the answer to Jane Griefly's death? Had she learnt of her father's villainy? Had she too killed herself? Who could have murdered her? Why? Could it possibly have been an accident? Was it even possible that Griefly had gone mad, and that he himself had pushed his own daughter to her doom – perhaps twistedly thinking her partly responsible for the shame she was bringing on the proud little family by her pregnancy? These questions oscillated between the three of us. We decided that she had definitely been killed – for a heartless girl such as she was would not have thought of suicide just because she had, for example, perhaps come to know that her father was a murderer. Then who killed her? Why? There was plenty of data on which to work: was there any significance in Mr. Edward's presence at the bridge? had he come to see if he had left any clues, made any slips? had he indeed ever been Jane's lover? Was there anything in Mr. Ramon's presence in the tower? and what had he to do with the Grieflys, except that he was friendly with them, lived in a cottage in their immediate vicinity, and had been charming to Mrs. Griefly in her trouble – Mrs. Dod had told us. Did this present an angle? Had Mrs.Griefly got a hidden pile of money, or something equally romantic? or was the wretched Ramon in love with her?

However we looked at the case, we could arrive at no satisfactory conclusion. George and I decided that since we had progressed so far so successfully, no stone would remain unturned till we had discovered the murderer, solved the whole mystery, and, what was most important, had set free the innocent Cummings senior.

Lunch ended, George went to bed; he always did on a

The Letters

Sunday afternoon. Mrs. Gifford said she was "very busy"; she bustled hither and thither preparing her room, her table, her food, and then herself, all for the afternoon to which the Thompsons had been invited. I helped as well as I could, but mainly hindered. At last all was ready, and Mrs. Cranford sat down to await her guests. I promptly put to one side the paper I'd been reading, and took the opportunity of talking to Dora, for there had been so little time in the last two days for so delightful an occupation.

"Are you tired?" I asked.

"No, of course not," she replied touching her hair, as only a woman can, and enquiring, anxiously, "Why? do I look tired?"

"Good Heavens no," I assured her. "No, no, I just wondered. You never seem to stop working. You're always rushing round doing something."

She changed the subject: "Are you happy with George, Peter?"

"Yes, we have a lot in common; we're having a grand time. This morning we worked out a lot together. We'll find the murderer I'm sure – at least – I hope so."

Dora smiled, "What a strange Halt Bridge you've come back to, isn't it amazing?"

"What extraordinary things have happened. In peace-time I'd have been absolutely shaken, but now I just accept it as something that has come along, as just another situation to be dealt with. It's the war's influence. Yes, it's queer alright, but I like it."

"I went for a walk through the village this morning to see Jean. Peter – rumours are flashing round like wild-fire. Mrs. Dyers told me her maid had told her that Mr. Ramon had murdered all three, and Mrs. Henner thinks the whole thing's ridiculously obvious, that Griefly killed them both, but she doesn't say why. It's awfully funny, honestly Peter." As she spoke, I wondered how long

Sunday

the walk had been that she could meet not only Jean, but Mrs. Dyers and Mrs. Henner. She continued, "And so it goes on. Really, Peter, the whole village is alive with murder talk, and they're all looking suspiciously at each other – they even wonder what you're doing here."

"What, me?" I exclaimed.

"Yes, Peter, don't look so annoyed. I heard one group talking about you."

"What did they say?" I asked.

"Well, they thought it was strange how you got into the church-yard this morning. And queer, too, how you arrived at Halt Bridge at just such a time as this."

"My! my! So I'm under suspicion, eh? That's just perfect. Oh boy!"

Dora said, "Here they are."

"Who?" I asked, a little confused. "Where?"

"The Thompsons of course," she laughed.

"Oh!" I said blankly, and thought, 'How like a woman!'

George was wakened. Tea was a great success with Jean, Bart, Bill their son and heir, and his fiancée Angela. (Beryl was not present, as she had an engagement with Capt. Ebbse.)

After tea Bill and Angela went for a walk together, at Jean's suggestion; Jean and Dora stayed talking by the fireside, whilst Bart, George, and I went for a short walk towards the farm at the top of the hill behind No. 5.

I walked a little behind the other two, since there was not room for us three abreast. George looked very small beside Bart – tall, massive-shaped like a triangle, the base of which were his shoulders. He kept turning back towards me, passing a friendly remark; when he spoke he seemed to smile, his pale blue eyes twinkling out of his kindly, strong, whimsical face. I watched his white hair showing handsomely beneath his hat. On reaching a point about half way up the hill George stopped.

"I want to try to contact a man here. You know Bart – Mr. Baker. I seem to remember him a year or so ago being very intimately acquainted with Jane Griefly. Do you?"

Bart said he didn't, at the same time intimating that he was not going to be dragged into some hair-brain scheme – he recalled, he said, the time he had saved the situation in the case of the stolen Maddock gate, and he did not want anything like that to occur again.

George, declaring that he'd had nothing to do with the gate anyway (he'd instigated the whole idea, but had taken no active part in the actual transport of the gate. Incidentally, he'd violently disapproved when he saw trouble rearing its frightful head. But even the greatest men sometimes falter!), said to me, "We must interview this man Baker."

So this was the reason for George's uphill walk!

I nodded, and we moved on upwards, talking of this and that.

Our sudden, and surprising encounter with Mr. Baker left Bart and I dumbfounded. A little more than halfway up the path was a gate leading to Baker's farm. Our heads bent in our climb, we did not at first notice the figure leaning against this gate; the figure was Baker's. George was our leader and behaved as such. "Good evening, Baker," he said quickly.

Mr. Baker took his pipe out of his mouth, looked at each of us in turn, replaced the pipe, and said, "Evening."

George appeared a little startled at these tactics, but leaning jauntily on his stick at such an angle that I thought he must fall over,

Sunday

he said, "My word, Baker – exciting news in the village, eh?"

Mr. Baker, still leaning on the gate, puffed at his pipe unperturbed. He wore a dirty cap on the back of his black, rough hair; a man of medium height, a broad-shouldered farmer, he had a face like a fox. His manner in this miniature crisis was one of insolent defiance to anybody or anything which might have reason to approach him on whatever subject.

Mr. Thompson and I glanced sideways at each other, as if to say, 'What next?'

Mr. Baker spoke briefly, "There's news enough in the world to-day." His accent was Northern; I noticed the sing-song of his words. His remark impressed George, who applied the ignoble art of flattery. "By Jove, man, you're about the first sensible person I've met in the village. They all seem to have forgotten themselves and the purpose of our lives to-day, just because of a local blood-shed. Ridiculous!"

Mr. Baker made no comment. Bart nudged me; when I looked at him he winked.

"Mrs. Griefly must be very upset." – It was Bart who had spoken.

Mr. Baker said surprisingly, "Mrs. Griefly's all right."

"How do you mean?" I asked.

"I mean she's alright," replied Mr. Baker conclusively.

George, whose silence had become a mystery, said with dramatic force, as though after a lot of thought he had come to a quick decision, "I sympathise with you, Baker. I remember you were very fond of Jane, weren't you?" George was triumphant.

Bart wanted, to walk back, but George insisted we should continue to the top of the hill, returning by the road, "Otherwise," he said, "Baker will know for certain that I tried to tackle him."

We had, I thought, gained very little from our short encounter, except that Jane Griefly's name did have a remarkable effect on Baker, which certainly made him a suspect along with Edwards.

"Had Jane Griefly any other lovers? can you remember – Bart?" asked George.

"Can't say I remember any particular one. She's had so many," replied Bart with a smile.

"Yes, I mean earnest love affairs, ones lasting several months or so," George amended.

"Ah well," said Bart, "there's that young fellow – I can't say I like him myself – what's his name? Flashy clothes, rabbity, thin! what do they call him? something to do with Delilah –"

"Samson?" I asked.

"That's it," laughed George, "you've guessed it, Peter, and vou're right, Bart – that young ruffian was about with the girl for a long while. Hmm!"

"But where," I asked, "is this getting us? what motives have any of these men, except perhaps passionate anger, or something as simple as that?"

Bart wisely pointed out that the simple answers were nearly always the correct ones.

We began to plod down the steep hill leading into Halt Bridge from the North.

"Why look who's here!" I cried as we came to a bend in the road, showing the long stretch to the level-crossing at the bottom. Pushing his bicycle, and tramping slowly up was a figure in blue.

"Ah! Now! – my Javert, here comes the blundering police force," said George with that laugh which at parties made

Sunday

everybody smile; Bart and I smiled.

"Let's tackle him, Javert. What say you, Bart?"

"You be careful what you're doing with old Stott. He's a nasty customer. You don't want to get yourself into trouble, George," advised Bart, always the steady, the resourceful.

"Don't worry, Bart. We'll deal with him, eh, Peter ?"

George was in the highest spirits, but I said, "I think I'd better watch my step this time, don't you?"

"By Jove, you had," said he. "Leave everything to me."

As we came level with the village's Arm of the Law, George greeted it with, "Good evening to you, Stott. Still hard at work?"

The arm of the Law halted with a puff, and said 'Good evening.'

"Yes Mr. Cranford. Just let loose Ramon," he murmured gloomily. Things obviously had not been going well with the constable, so George thought this a discreet moment to tell him of our morning's work, discoveries, and theories.

"I've got some theories on all this, which will surprise you," said George with energy, "revolutionary theories!"

"Oh," said the Arm of the Law without enthusiasm, but glad to listen, having a rest from his laborious climb. George outlined our investigations in detail. He finished by saying, "Well, Stott, what do you think? are you interested?"

There was a long silence. P.C. Stott stood very still, holding his bike in front of him. At last he spoke: "I advise you gentlemen not to meddle in matters which you are not qualified to look into. I strongly advise you to watch what you say in the future. I've had about enough, what with him (nodding in my direction) this morning, and your wasting my time with your talk!" He jerked his head

The Letters

vigorously to indicate that the discussion had come to an end; and trundled his bicycle on up the hill.

After we had recovered from our surprise, I was all for telling him what we thought of him, but Bart started to walk down.

Bart said, "That fellow's too big for his boots. I've never heard such ill-mannered behaviour before."

I said, "I'd like to knock that cap of his over his ugly fat face."

George said, "By gad, Bart! By Jove, man! We'll see! I'll make him look so small! He can't do this to me! I've never met such impertinence in my life before! Peter, you – and I – we'll show him up. My word!" – and in this way he led the conversation until we reached the sympathetic Dora, who managed to ease his wrath with her feminine understanding, and such words as, "Ee, George! what an unpleasant man."

We spent a quiet evening in the upstairs sitting-room at the Blaydon Hotel, where we talked, drank, and danced, while Bill played the piano. So ended another day, but what an eventful one! what tragedy! what triumph! what changing mood!

That night I found even greater difficulty getting to sleep, for although I was tired, our problems tumbled before my eyes, a fantasia of jumbled nonsense. 'Would the jig-saw puzzle of Sidley ever fit together?' I wondered. And still wondering I fell asleep.

CHAPTER IV: BURGLARY - MONDAY

What a gathering of the clans! and at such an hour of the morning! What a cold morning! There was ice on the station platform. How sleepy we should have been! Yet how wide awake we were! What strange circumstances! The time was half past eight, and the awaited train from Carlisle was due in a few minutes.

A wisp of mist covered the far side of the valley and the distant houses; a shimmering haze smoked gently from the moving river face; it was freezing cold. I stamped my feet vigorously and clapped my hands together to keep warm; but my mind, my attention, was not concentrated on physical matters, I was listening intently to the confused voices which heralded more news, new developments over night.

'This is amazing,' I thought. 'Things are moving a bit too fast for me. I'd hardly credit what's happening, the speed, the strangeness of it all, and the complication. How can we hope to sort it all out? Will things never stop?'

Lined up on Halt Bridge station were Mr. and Mrs. Thompson (Bart going to work in Newcastle, Jean going in to be with Dora for the day), Bill and Angela (both going back to their Hospital where they worked), Beryl (who would be leaving us at Hentham for her A.R.P. functions!), Mr. and Mrs. Cranford (George going in to make arrangements at his office about his holiday, Dora taking the opportunity for a day in town with her husband), and myself (who was a sort of hanger-on, whom the family felt they could hardly leave behind). We were all talking about the latest only event, although only Bill knew anything about it!

The train thundered out of the mist, chugged to a standstill, and proceeded to hiss and chunter ominously. We all managed to scramble into one compartment, sitting down amidst great confusion. Fortunately there was nobody else in the carriage; and we were able to keep the coach to ourselves all the way, even after Beryl had left us. As the bustle died down, Bart made the remark simultaneously with Jean that the men had all sat on one side, and the ladies on the other; this we thought to be a great joke, and when the laughter in its turn died away, the atmosphere changed to one of intense drama.

George said, "Now Bill! Tell us the story right from the very beginning. It is most important to us, because it throws a new light on the matter – or rather, it confirms one of our theories – that a lover is at the bottom of all this – At least, I think it does. But let –"

"George!" Dora interrupted gently. "Let Bill tell his story then. Don't you try to do it."

George gave Dora a withering look, and we all laughed.

"Yes? – Bill?" he said majestically intimating that Bill might proceed with his tale whenever he chose.

Bill leaned forward, delving into the vast pockets of his overcoat for his pipe. His ginger hair was neatly brushed and parted, his glasses gave his face a very serious expression, but his blue eyes twinkled whimsically like Bart's, indeed he was a young and slender replica of his massive father. With a smile on his face, he looked round at his audience – Dora and Jean were already whispering and smiling benevolently to each other about their respective flock, so he cautioned them with a frown.

"Well, I went to bed last night in the normal way, and fell asleep almost at once."

I looked towards Angela, physically the exact opposite to her fiancée, a well-built, tall girl with a round face, pale blue eyes; she gazed steadily at Bill, even more intently than did George. I thought how quietly attractive, how very sweet she was.

Bill puffed his pipe into action as he lighted it, the fumes filled the confined space with a manly smell, and Jean coughed

Monday

disgustedly. Jean had her pretty head cocked to one side in an attitude of pride and admiration: Jean was the Mother, whom all the boys loved, and to whom without fail they all told their troubles and gave their sincerest confidences; Jean was loved by all.

"By Jove, Bill – that pipe's taking a long time to light," said George impatiently.

We laughed.

Angela said, "Come on, Bill," and the Mothers twittered their impatience. Bill and I exchanged uncouth winks, which Beryl observed and betrayed. There was a clucking of conversation, terminated by George's remark, "Well, I really don't know – I thought – I thought – we were about to hear – from Bill here – his exciting – "

"George! George!" We all shouted. Just as we were settling down once more for the adventure-story, the train chuffed into Hentham and tall, graceful Beryl slithered from our midst into the murky outside. After the farewells George was obviously ready to say something of importance, but Bill continued.

"I couldn't have been asleep very long, when I woke with a start, and sat up. Something had disturbed me; a noise, I believe. The sound was repeated. It was a scream, a woman's scream – and quite close. Without bothering to put on a dressing gown, or anything, I dashed outside to see what was the matter.

"There came a clatter of breaking glass, followed by a heavy thud in the direction of the fat woman's cottage. As I ran down the pathway, I saw a dark figure running at full speed away from the house. It was a man, but I couldn't make out who it was, or what he was wearing; it was too dark. He was only a few yards away from me, but the garden gate was shut, and by the time I had opened it, he had jumped down the bank into the river and was wading along towards the Blaydon. He must have known the river well, because as I followed, he splashed out across at just the right place – where there's a shallow passage to the other side – the only spot for many

The Letters

yards around where you can get over without going down waist-deep or having to swim. It was dark, and when I got to the other side, he had disappeared.

"Whilst this was happening I could hear the shouts from the cottage, 'Help me, help me! Oh dear, troubles come by hundreds. Oh help! Oh help!'"

"Bill – did she really say those words?" interrupted Jean. "How could you hear from the other side of the river? I didn't even hear in the Cottage."

There was a terrible silence. Then ignoring his Mother, Bill continued to the accompaniment of stifled feminine giggles.

"I went back to quieten the old lady. When I got there a number of cottagers had arrived to help her, and she was quiet. Mrs. Dod was there too.

"This is the queer part – when I first dashed out after the man, I thought I had seen a female form standing near the cottage gate, but I can't be sure, and at the time I was too busy chasing the chap. I asked her now, what she was doing up at this time of night, and she said, 'I couldn't sleep. I've been worrying rather about my John. He's stationed in one of the blitzed areas. I thought I'd have a walk about. When I heard these screams, I was fairly near, so I came down to see what I could do'. Those weren't her exact words, but she. said something like that." Bill glared at his Mother, to drive home this point. Then he went on, "Anyway I told the old lady – it was Mrs.Griefly of all people – what I knew, and asked if she was O.K. and what had happened. She said, 'I was woke by a noise, and I saw a man come into me bedroom. I screamed and he took no notice but started emptyin' me drawers like he was lookin' for somethin'. He found them letters and went, breaking a window and I screamed for help all the time. I thank you for troublin' like this, Sir, and I am allright now thanks to all these kind people.'

"I stopped her going into an account of kindness bestowed on her during the past few days, and asked what letters had been

Monday

taken, and if she had lost anything else. She said, 'No, I've only had them letters took. They were letters what Jane had kept from one of her specials – I don't know who, but she was a one with the boys.'

"I was only just in time, extracting this information, because up rode P.C. Stott on his bicycle, which meant I had no bed for a long time, because he wanted full particulars, which he wrote out laboriously in his note-book. However, I at last got back into the Cottage, where I dried myself. Mother was up, though nobody else had wakened, and she made me some tea."

When he ended his modest tale, he puffed strenuously at his pipe, whilst we showered idiotic questions upon him as the train steamed on: had he any idea where the man went to? who he was? why had he done it? what time it was? what was Mrs. Dod doing? what did P.C. Stott say? was the water cold? was he tired? He answered these as well as he was able, and we thanked him, and praised him as heartily as he deserved; he was not grateful as we might have expected, for Bill hated this kind of attention; and I could see that Angela admired him for it.

Blaydon reached, we all began to feel drowsy, for Bart would not allow the windows to be opened and Bill's pipe combined with the compartment's heater created a very thick fug.

I shut my eyes and began to muse. 'What a story!' I thought. 'We've some more thinking to do. Who would risk such an action for a bundle of letters, but the alleged murderer? Why should he take such a risk? What was the content of those letters? Could we possibly find out what our various suspects were doing at that time of night? and Mrs. Dod, surely her statement was correct, or was it? It seemed definite now that we could say of our murderer – 'You are a man, because you were Jane Griefly's lover – you are well acquainted with Halt Bridge (assuming that you were the burglar), because on a dark night you were able to make your way at speed through the shallow Tyne bed with its treacherous deeps – and, you will be confident now that the last piece of damning evidence, which nobody had thought about except yourself, has comes into your

The Letters

possession, and which you have probably destroyed! So although the plot thickens, there is some more light upon it. I wonder what will happen next? Nothing will surprise me now!' – Jean and Dora rose to their feet saying, "We killed Jane Griefly for a joke."

I started violently for I had almost fallen asleep; as I hazily stood up, I saw that Dora and Jean were already standing, smiling together, pointing at me.

"Are you suspecting us of murder, Peter?" Jean asked.

"Good Heavens!" I cried sleepily. "How did you guess?"

Jean laughed. "Now Peter!" she said, "was that kind?"

I looked at the others. They had all wakened. The windows were open, cold air was rushing in. We were in Newcastle.

Within a few minutes we were all out of the carriage, off the platform and outside the station, where once more we clustered before parting. Bill and Angela left us first; we should not see them again until the next week-end.

"Good hunting, George," said Bill, and aside to me, "Look after him, Peter."

Angela dragged him away saying, "Goodbye, I hope you'll have the murderer under lock and key when we next see you."

I said, "Goodbye, yes we shall! You'll see."

George and Bart then left to attend their different functions; but we arranged to meet them at Fullers for lunch. Dora and Jean decided they had a lot of shopping to do, so I asked them if they would excuse my going up to the Hospital, as I had a dressing which needed attention. They agreed, sympathised, and departed; so I was the only one left there. In deep thought, I crossed to the tram stop in the centre of the street.

An agreeable lunch, a ludicrous picture show, a delightful

Monday

tea party at Tillys; and we returned to Halt Bridge tired and happy.

I escorted Jean back to the Cottage, whilst George and Dora returned to No. 5, George to contemplate the products of our weekend investigations, Dora to prepare a most lavish meal. I dilly-dallied talking to Beryl for a long time, so that it was past eight before I returned to the Cranfords' where there was food, hot and ready for immediate consumption.

At the end of supper, George, swallowing his last cup of tea, said;

"Well, Peter – to work –"

"No, George, Peter's tired. You can't go out now. It's late," said Dora.

"I'm fine, Mrs. Cranford, honestly," I pleaded. "We've got a lot to find out. After all, we've almost a whole day's information to track down, and devour."

She smiled sweetly, "Alright, but you won't mind if I go off to bed early, will you? I'm a little tired myself – a long day in Newcastle always makes me feel like that. I'll leave the kettle on the fire, and the tea-pot and things out in case you want some tea, when you come back. It's a very cold night, you know. Wrap up again, won't you?"

I thanked her for what she had said: she is one of the sweetest, kindest, most sympathetic, and charmingly feminine women I have ever met; she is also one of the prettiest, and most elegant.

I don't know why we chose to visit the Blaydon Hotel that night, possibly because of Mrs Dod's mysterious association with last night's story, or possibly because I wanted to see if there was any mail for me; anyway, George and I arrived there just after nine o'clock. As we entered, I rang the copper bell loudly to herald our arrival traditionally.

The Letters

May tittered, and said, "Good evening, sir." May was Mrs. Dod's maid. She opened the door leading to the room under the stairs, where we found Mrs. Dod seated interestedly on the wooden sofa next to a peculiar little man; the stranger was tapping energetically with his fingers on a typewriter. Mrs. Dod stood up as we came in.

"Hallo, Mrs. Dod," I shouted. "How are you after your adventure last night?"

She smiled naturally, saying, "Oh! a little tired, pet. And how did you enjoy yourself to-day?"

"We had a great time, saw an awful film!" I answered.

"Oh dear, I'm forgetting my manners," exclaimed Mrs. Dod, as she proceeded to introduce us to the individual with the typewriter, who she explained was a newspaper reporter staying the night here – a Mr. Prattle, who looked like a ferret.

"Mrs. Dod," said George firmly, "may we have – er – something to drink, eh? and you sir," he added addressing the ferret, "What's yours?"

"Thanks," said the ferret, "mine's a tot."

George looked at him sideways, then asked me, "And you, Peter?"

"The usual please."

George turned to Mrs. Dod and asked her if she "would partake of a spot" with him, but she laughed saying, "Oh no I don't touch it." She spoke with a strong Northumbrian accent, which was very pretty to hear.

"What! no whiskey?" I asked teasingly.

"Naughty boy!" she said, departing for the drinks.

Monday

She disappeared, leaving us alone with the monotonous rat-tat-tat of the typewriter. Sitting back in the hard little chair, I looked round the room; it was just the same as before – tiny. The slant of the stairs, the door, and steps formed one end; while a long window which looked out onto the river directly beneath gave one the impression, during day-light, of being in a large boat.

George said, "You've got a lot to write about, haven't you?"

"Yep, it's uncky. Bit o'jam. Lucky to get the job," replied the ferret with a significant twitch of his nose.

"Do you believe Cummings is – ah – guilty?" asked George.

"Oh yes, it's obvious. Bloke admits going out with Miss What's-her-name to the bridge, even says he had a row with her. Says something about leaving her, and regretting his temper. Returning again he found her gone. He must be potty to expect us to believe that sort of thing."

I noted the way he said 'us' when he meant 'the police'.

"That's very interesting," said George. "I wonder why he should have said that?"

Then turning his head towards me, he casually remarked, "You see, Peter. She was pushed over by 'X', who must have been lurking in the shadows previously, while Cummings walked off. If he went far enough the running water would probably have drowned any cry which the girl might have given. Obviously she wouldn't be there when he did return I – er wonder if there's more to the story than that."

"Coo," said the ferret. "You don't believe all that, do you? Silly! He's done it. It's just too obvious."

"That's where you're right," added George. "It's just too obvious."

The ferret smiled in a friendly manner at George, as May

The Letters

came in with the drinks. "Good health," he said. "Look. Since you're so interested, and I like your face, try this," and he jerked a piece of paper before George's eyes in a way which suggested that George should read what was written.

"It's some notes I took from the Inspector, a friend of mine – after the interviews were over," explained the ferret.

"What interviews?" I asked.

"Oh! They've been on all the day. Police asking question of all who had got entangled as it were. You know, routine job, getting all the dame's lover-johnnies taped – and some others too," he said with a coarse wink.

When George had finished reading the notes, he passed them over to me. Written clearly, they showed the alibis of the people questioned concerning the burglary – as follows:

Halt Bridge Burglary   Date   Time 1.30 a.m.

J.B. Ramon - Age: 37 years. Farmer. Said asleep, knew nothing of the burglary till next day – No proof.

A.G. Dod - Age: ? Proprietress, 'Blaydon Hotel'. Said unable to sleep, because worried about husband, decided to go for a walk about 1.30 a.m. Saw X chased by Thompson's boy. Helped Mrs.Griefly. Went to bed.

F.M. Baker - Age: 26 years. Farmer. Said went to bed early ready for Monday's work. No proof.

J.K. Samson - Age 23 years. Clerk. Said at dance at Hentham, missed the train back. But a witness saw him return on a motor bike. Pays fine for contempt of court. Under suspicion.

C.J. Edwards - Age: 27 years. Lieutenant in local Tank unit. Said was visiting girl friend at the top of North Hill. Left her about 1 a.m.

Monday

"Mumm!" I said when I read the notes. "They all looks suspicious, don't they?"

"Oh yes, it's always like that. It's the Devils own job. The Samson kid got into proper trouble with his lying."

"Yes, I'll bet he did. I wonder what he's got to do with this. I must have a word with young Samson," said George grimly.

We talked. We drank another round which I paid for. Deciding it was getting late, we returned to No. 5, bidding all, the ferret included, a very good evening.

"We have luck, Peter, don't we?" said George, as we walked back.

"You're right, we're darned lucky, but as far as I can see, things are even more sticky. You know the motives are the things we want to sort out. I mean, what for instance would Ramon have to do with it? I think he's sound enough don't you?"

"I'm not sure. Never liked the man, as I've said before. But what about Mrs. Dod? I think it's ridiculous even to consider her. What say you?"

"Mumm!" I murmured. "However, the other three are problems, aren't they? Baker seems the least likely. I can't think what this chap Samson's been up to, can you?"

"No, but I'll see about him myself," George assured.

"Well, that leaves Edwards. He's got something to explain. It would take about half an hour to get round to the cottage from way up on the hillside there, wouldn't it? What do you think?" I asked.

"Yes he's got something to explain, man, but if he had planned the burglary – which I'm sure X did – then he would have fitted himself up with a suitable alibi, wouldn't he?"

"Yes, I suppose he would," I agreed, "Oh dear, this is getting nowhere. Now why should Baker want to murder the girl? or Edwards for that matter? or Samson? I tell you unless it was done in a fit of passion, there's no way to look at it. And if it comes to passion any of them might have done it."

"But what of this piece of information about Cummings' story? A story which I believe."

We had reached No. 5, and I opened the door for George.

"Thank you," he said. "The jealous lover must have followed the two of them out to Sidley, eh? Now who would do such a thing? Surely not just a lover? I wonder."

"We're up against brains of a sort, as you say," I admitted, "and we're sinking deeper into the mire. At each fresh discovery, each piece of news we are heartened, but when we look into it we find the puzzle even more complex than before."

"Never worry," said the great man willfully. "Be strong. We shall win through. Never fear."

The kettle was boiling on the fire, so we thought we would have tea before retiring. As we made the tea, I remembered that I had forgotten to ask Mrs. Dod if there was any mail for me, and mentioned the fact to George.

"Peter, man," he said. "What's this? The great detective has not failed in so trivial a matter, surely? eh, Javert?"

"What do you mean?" I laughed.

"I mean," said George solemnly, "that you should realise that if there had been any mail for you, Mrs. Dod would have given it to you. Do you see? Eh?"

I saw, but I answered, "Well, I forgot to ask if there was any mail. Isn't it conceivable that – supposing there had been some – Mrs. Dod might also have forgotten to give it to me?"

Monday

"Oh no, that's too much for me at this time of night, and by Jove it's getting on for eleven. We've had a busy day."

We drank our tea, and after a short discussion of the film we had seen, went up to bed.

Another day of excitement had passed. As I got into bed, I considered what to-morrow would bring – if there would be any more adventures. What a strange life I had returned to! I liked it. What happy surroundings for it all! It was grand, although there was that cloud in the shape of the imprisoned man. If only I was more confident that cloud could be driven away! Was George thinking similarly next door? Listening hard, I heard a heavy snoring; it was my answer.

Still thinking, I went to sleep.

CHAPTER V: MR GRIEFLY'S LETTER - TUESDAY

George and I were seated at the breakfast table. Dora was hurrying about, as though she expected Mr. Churchill himself to pay her a visit later in the day. George was looking through the local paper, the 'Hentham Gazette'; we had ordered this daily, so as to have all fresh developments and police reports concerning the tragedies as soon as they were available. I glanced through the 'Telegraph' for news of the Desert War. It was a peaceful scene. The room glowed with the dancing yellow reflections from the spritely, crackling fire, as it burned merrily in the grate. On the windows clung frost; and outside, the air was ice-cold. I felt warm, comfortable, happy.

George suddenly grunted. Laying his paper on the table before him, he indiscriminately pushed plates in all directions to make room.

"At last," he said, then paused. I looked at him with amazement. Had the chase started so early this morning? What had he read? He was muttering again.

"They've been hiding it from us. No wonder we made no headway. We're getting somewhere now."

"Where," I asked, "are we getting? What goes on? Won't you let me in on this?"

In reply George rustled the paper about, slapped his hand noisily at a certain paragraph, and said, "Read that, man. See how these police have tried to thwart us. See how they have withheld valuable information."

He began to muse, and spoke to himself rather than to me, "A letter – yes, letters – the whole thing revolves on letters – if only I could get that missing link – letters, that's the answer."

Tuesday

"What's all this?" I asked.

"Have you read that, man?" George questioned me by way of an answer.

I hurriedly began reading, and said, "Not quite."

The paragraph contained a brief police summary of the course of events since last Friday night, together with a letter which had been written by Mr. Griefly just before his death. I looked quickly at George, then stared back at the letter there in print. It was headed and worded as follows:

"To Whoever should read this in the police-station: Date..........

"I cannot write good but I write what is true and tell all I know before I go to my death. My daughter Jane writes her notes to her lads and sends them by some tradesmen but I dont know who it is but he picks up her notes from a hole in the outside of the garden wall. I saw her put a note there one day that is how I know I took it and read it. It said something like Meet me at the usual place at six o'clock when we can talk about a awful thing what's come to me – a little stranger. I felt horrid when I read that. I saw red. I did not tell Lora my wife but I changed the time and place. I forge her writing easy because it is not far off mine and I put the note back where I found it. I goes to Sidley Bridge the place I had wrote early because it is dark and I dont want to miss him. When he comes he is surprised like when he finds me and I tells him what I know and he swears horrible saying she has been in secret with somebody else. I lose my temper. I calls him a liar and I hit him and knock him down and when I think what he done I see red and pick up a rock from the river and hit him hard on the back of the head. I sees I killed him so I dont panic. I throw the rock in the river and I think I will make it look like an accident by throwing him in front of a car. I drag him up the bank away from the corner where people sometimes wait for the bus. I leave him by a tree and look for a gap in the hedge. Soon I hear music which is the noise of tanks coming up the road. I find

The Letters

a thin bit of hedge and drag the corpse ready. I hold it up and let it drop when the first tank comes. The tanks stop and I scoot it off home quick down by the river. My folks dont wonder where I been because I get a pint at the Dutch first and they smell I been there. Then came Jane's end. I think I am going barmy. I see that Sidley Bridge in my sleep first him and then her who I love and it was all for nothing. I keep seeing that bridge, that bridge all the day. I am not stopping I am leaving everything to Lora. She won't mind so long as I leave her set up. I have said all that matters in good reason but I am going barmy and I will kill myself to save Lora the sorrow of me being daft. I can't face this horrible sight of the bridge and the dark and that corpse and the noise of the tanks and the noise and that big bridge and them two corpses my Jane and at Sidley Bridge where she used to carry her tea of an afternoon with her friends. That bridge is always with me. I have said all I need."

When I had finished reading, I said, "My, my, well, that's one in the eye for P.C. Stott, isn't it? It's just exactly what we said. Boy oh boy! this is good!"

George was serious. "Yes," he said, "the whole thing rests on letters."

"What do you mean?"

"I mean – that a letter caused the death of young Cummings – letters were the reason for a daring and successful burglary – a letter has shown us the way more clearly – and there will be more letters before we finish – a bundle of letters, if we find who is 'X'."

I frowned, "A bundle of letters?"

George smiled a smile, which I could see was meant to be sinister. "Wait and see, Peter. Wait till we find our X, Peter."

Ignoring George's act, I re-read Griefly's letter. "Mr. Cranford?" I said.

"Javert?" said George.

Tuesday

"What strikes me most in that letter is one phrase. This one," and I read out the words, "'She has been in secret with somebody else.'"

George nodded his head sternly.

"Those are the words Griefly alleges the sailor to have said. Did the sailor know something about Jane do you think? – 'in secret with somebody else' – I wonder."

George smiled, "Yes, we're really getting somewhere now – between us. You're right. You're quite right – that phrase coupled with my letters – that'll do the trick."

I smiled in return, but was very puzzled by his words. 'Had he,' I thought, 'really got something up his sleeve?'

George abruptly said, "We have work to do. We must see Samson and Edwards to-day. We may find out something. There are but few links missing now, Peter. How about it? Let's go out to the Cottage first and see if we can't manufacture – an excuse from there." He frowned with one eyebrow and laughed with his eyes, "An excuse for a visit to the Castle. Eh? – What say you?"

"When does the drink come in?" I asked.

"What! Already, man?" George said in astonishment. "Later, man, later, we'll take our quaff, what?"

Walking towards the bridge George and I happened to pass P.C. Stott, who looked very dignified.

"Good morning, Stott. Have you seen Griefly's letter?" George asked fiercely. P.C. Stott, making believe not to have heard, turned about and tinkered with the rear wheel of his bicycle, as though there was something wrong with it.

I called over my shoulder, "Well, if you want to be put on the right track about anything just come to us; we'll be only too willing to oblige."

P.C. Stott stood savagely to his feet and glared at an unfortunate child passing in front of him.

"Now then, man, don't go too far," George warned me. "There's not long to wait now. We've only got to make up our minds who's done the murder, for I'm sure it's murder, and I can fix the rest."

I was becoming suspicious of these extraordinary remarks, and said as much.

"Well, man, who has done it?" he asked in reply. What a question! I said nothing.

George startled me by suddenly saying, "Peter, I am serious. From now – until the kill (a word, which he spoke with relish) – we shall employ some new – and I am sure – effective – tactics. Listen – we are going to bluff our way forwards with our suspects, till we get results. Mind you, none of them may have had anything to do with it. On the other hand, a group of them may have worked it together – but I doubt it very much."

He paused for breath, and I nodded my head approvingly, murmuring, "Umm."

"We shall use trickery – to our own ends. We shall be as the Jesuits, and our end – the release of an innocent man – will justify the means, which we shall engage. Eh, Peter? Eh, Javert? but no, Javert would have none of that – I must call you – Peter." This was said melodramatically, with his stick held aloft, a gesture, which some village shoppers eyed suspiciously.

At the Cottage we found Mrs. Thompson busy washing some of Bart's socks. Witnessing our entry, she became coyly embarrassed, but George masterfully said, "By Jove Mrs. Thompson, Bart's a lucky man to have such a wife – my word!"

Before we left the artful George had won all that we required, and we left Jean Thompson on an errand to the Castle;

Tuesday

we were to invite Ebbse and Edwards to the Cottage for tea that afternoon.

We walked on up the hill between banks of barren trees; we listened to the trickling hillside stream which ran beneath the road; and we moved quickly to keep ourselves warm. As we reached the flat part of the road at the top of the first climb, we looked out across the Tyne to the green hills rising backwards into the distance, to the grey shapes of cottages, which were farms, to the shapeless distant stones, which were derelict mines, to the winding yellow trails, which were the desolate tracks leading far away up to the gigantic ridge – to Hadrians Wall. George decided to rest for a moment, so we leaned against a three-bar fence, which joined the ends of two walls, grey stone walls of neatly erected boulders, which one sees everywhere in Northumberland, dividing the wastes into sectors.

George was talking politics, or rather he was talking Churchill, that indomitable figure, the hero of all George's ideals. He savagely executed a plant with his stick to emphasise a point.

In the distance I saw a "spitfire" silhouetted against the grey-white cloudless sky; it dipped its wings from side to side and dived like a playing salmon; when it came closer, its background changed, the hillside showing behind it, so that it seemed almost to be floating in a void held there in the valley. The Spitfire disappeared, and we resumed our course towards Alsley.

Alsley Castle is one of many North Country fortresses. Tall and grey, seen from the opposite hills, it looks like a fairy palace nestling there in the woods. We climbed the grass slopes leading to the main entrance, stumbled past a number of tanks, and were about to enquire the whereabouts of Capt. Ebbse, when we heard again the laugh, which had startled us at Sidley the day before yesterday. Turning, we saw flabby Edwards leaning out of the turret of his tank.

He laughed, "On the war-path again, Mr. Blake? or is it Holmes? Yes, my God –" He laughed more loudly as an idea came

The Letters

to him. "It's not Blake at all, is it? It must be Holmes – because of the clinging Watson."

I blushed furiously. George ignoring his remarks, said, "Good morning. I have a communication for you from Mrs. Thompson, who has invited Capt. Ebbse and yourself to tea at the Cottage this afternoon. Beryl has the afternoon off-ah."

Edwards laughed rudely again. "That's a good excuse to come round asking a bloke questions, isn't it? I've brains, Mr. Cranford," he said, stressing the 'Mr'.

"By Jove, you're an impudent puppy!" George was angry, and said more than he had possibly intended, "but you're in a fix – ah – in a fix, by Jove. And you'll it find it difficult explaining how you were – so close to the scene – of the burglary, when it occurred."

I watched Edwards as George spoke. He became serious, a worried sneer came to his face – 'It's because he's frightened,' I thought, 'he's scared of being accused, and having his military career damaged, but I can't believe he's really got anything to do with all this. He's too much of a rat to have the nerve to commit a murder.'

George went on, "You know you're in for it, don't you? We'll teach you for your insolence."

I had never before seen the Great Man so angry; his eyes became slits, and he tapped the ground with his walking stick.

Edwards scoffed nervously, "You can't bluff me, and you've got nothing against me. Keep out of my way. Look after your own business. And don't interfere with things that don't concern you. Anyway, haven't you anything better to do? There's a war on, you know."

We realised from these words that we had found out as much as was possible from a man of Edwards' character, so we quickly left. As we moved away, the voice called out from its tank:

Tuesday

"Thank Mrs. Thompson, and tell her I'll be coming, will you? – Ebbse too, I know he'll want to be with Beryl."

On the way back, we called on Jean to tell her whom to expect for tea; we looked up Mrs. Dod to collect a large parcel and some letters, which to my delight had arrived for me; and we visited Mrs. White, where we partook of some quaff before retiring to Dora and our luncheon.

Lunch was just ready when we got back.

"Well," asked Dora, "have you enjoyed yourselves this morning? have you found anything more, Peter? has George behaved himself?" She spoke eagerly.

George said, "Of course we have behaved ourselves, Dore –" There was a twinkle in the Great Man's eye. He winked at me with a confident sideways twist of his head, and cried in a dramatic voice – his hand raised clutching his battered trilby, "By Jove, Dora – but we've had a bit of trouble – eh, what? – Peter – what say you?"

I nodded my head, smiling, "Yes, Mrs. Cranford – that darned Edwards bloke! I've never met anyone quite so rude. It's incredible! This morning we –"

"Why what's he done, Peter?" Dora interrupted.

"What's he done?" repeated George outraged. "He's only laughed in our faces – made rude insinuations – told us to mind our own business – made us look fools in front of his men – an officer! – think of it, Dora – I've never been –" He suddenly remembered Edwards' last remark, so he changed the trend of his speech. "Then – Dora – then he had the cheek – the audacity – to accept our invitation!"

"But George!" Dora was confused; she appealed to me, as being possibly less 'moved' by the recent events. "Peter! What is all this? what's happened?"

When I had told her, she said, "Ee! What a rude man! I never really liked him. What a nasty thing to say!"

Lunch eaten, the conversation changed to the afternoon.

"Let's go for a walk by the river," suggested Dora brightly.

George said we had done enough walking for one day.

"What about Alston? It's lovely round there. What time are the 'Buses?" I asked.

George ignored the question; he thought the journey would be too cold.

"Well then," enquired Dora, "where do you want to go? Do you want to do anything, or not? because I've got a lot of work to do."

George was the 'Monarch of all he surveyed', and he was enjoying this lime-light. However, his attitude was likely to last so long as to entirely sabotage the afternoon's prospects; so I said suddenly – with a more decisive note than I had intended, "I know – we'll go to the 'George'. Why not?" So we went to the George.

The George is a pretty little hotel by the side of the Tyne at a place called Cholerford. White-washed walls, dark green firs, and unkempt lawns sloping to the water's edge enhanced the Inn nestling there in a valley, a peaceful, delightful place for tea, for quiet, for thought.

We arrived there at about four o'clock. I felt particularly happy: I had received a letter from my mother saying that she would probably be coming up on Wednesday or Thursday; mail had been received from Sheila; and the parcel from home contained my civilian clothes, so that I was now dressed as a free man. We sat at a tea table by a window from which we could see the wild garden, the bridge, and the river. Conversation concerned the effect of sudden death upon the inhabitants of Halt Bridge.

Tuesday

I began: "I've got a little theory, which is somehow relevant to what's going on now in the village, back at Halt, that is. Well, I've sort of called it the theory of 'acceptance and realisation'. Let me explain. How often do people who are 'not of the world' – say my mother for instance – accept a fact without having the imagination, the experience and the knowledge or the belief in it to realise it. Take as an example the terrible reports of the Nazi administration in Poland. Mother accepts these 'horror stories' in that she thinks they may possibly have occurred, but she treats them rather as a tale from the 'Arabian Nights'; she never realises the truth of them. Do you see what I mean?"

Mrs. Cranford nodded her head; George appeared to sleep.

"Well anyway, to get to the point," I continued, "Halt Bridge's attitude towards the war is like my mother's outlook on Nazi-committed Polish atrocities.

"The people of Halt Bridge will not face the facts, will not accept realities, will not get out of that sluggish mire of self-satisfaction into which they have fallen. They've got stamped at the back of their minds a very strong and commonly popular belief that 'it can't happen here'. You know it so well. Even after Dunkirk it was still prevalent. Even after the great cities had been hit and people began first to understand, it still remained. They knew Jerry intended to invade us; they knew it was possible; and yet they couldn't imagine it happening, so they would not actually accept the possibility. Isn't that true?"

Mrs. Cranford nodded her head; again George stirred.

"Well now," I said, speaking slowly, "in the recent local events we've seen the people moved. They've been more interested – why, they've even become suspicious of each other! You can see it in their faces. There's a definite atmosphere about Halt Bridge. Why? Why has the war taken second place to local deaths? Why have they forgotten their ideals, and hopes temporarily? Why is the war and war news driven from their

The Letters

thoughts and conversation? Go into any pub there, and you'll hear them talking of 'Jane Griefly', or 'that sailor' or 'Sidley Bridge', or 'Ramon', or any of the other names associated with the drama. Now why is that? It's because death is at their very doorstep; they're right next door to it; they've seen animation snuffed in violence overnight; they are a little bit afraid. They see further than just sensationalism. They think of themselves and of their own lives. They pray at night times now! Death on their doorstep – not a thousand deaths in the paper or on the radio. Because they are in some way feeling, or being affected by sudden death themselves they begin to understand, to see the meaning of blitzkrieg in everyday life. They feel now that 'it can happen here'. They have learnt a lesson, don't you agree? They are beginning to realise, and slowly they are changing, discarding mere acceptance. Yet when the memory of near violence has long past, they will sink back into their small-minded, jealous lives accepting coldly without realising at all."

"Peter, isn't that just a wee bit exaggerated?" asked Mrs. Cranford.

"Yes it is a little," I said with a smile. "Well anyway, that was rather long. You must excuse me, Mrs. Cranford – I seem to have outdone even George for the moment."

"Not at all, Peter," Mrs. Cranford said. "That was grand."

"My word, man, you can talk," commented George.

Suddenly George leaned forward, placed his elbows solemnly upon the table, and told us in full detail the terrible account of his days of fighting in France, of his comrades of war, until Mrs. Cranford interrupted him.

"Oh," she said, "look at the time."

We grabbed our coats, assisting each other into them. Then George paid the bill; Mrs. Cranford powdered her nose; and I snatched up the last cake.

Tuesday

It was in the Cottage on our return that Dora amused us with some information about the Halt Bridge ties. "Oh my," she said, "I forgot to tell you. I heard some awfully funny things this morning, when you were out."

"You seem, Dora," said George, "to spend your time hearing things."

"Don't be so silly, George. I went shopping, and met Mrs. Dod," Mrs. Cranford explained.

"Mrs. Dod!" I laughed. "Ah, there you have an Encyclopaedia! Whiskey hath charms!"

"Oh Peter – poor Mrs. Dod," smiled Mrs. Cranford. "Yes she told me she'd heard –"

"Well now," said George quite sharply, "and what did she hear?"

Unperturbed, Dora continued, "She said she'd heard that 'that girl Beryl wasn't past suspicion', that 'those evacuees' – meaning us and the Thompsons – 'were likely to have something to do with it, because they'd been here only a short time' – two years! short time! And what's more they suspect you two more than anybody else, especially you, Peter."

"What!" George and I said together – we 're suspected? Go on, what is it?"

Dora smiled, "All right. Well – they said –"

"Who said?" George asked.

"Look, George, do you, or don't you want me to tell you about it?"

"Do go on, Mrs. Cranford," I pleaded.

"Well – the people in the village said they thought it was

The Letters

funny that you two had got nothing better to do than go round asking people questions. You see, they've noticed you. And you, Peter! They wonder what you're doing here, because they know this isn't your home, and they know Sheila isn't here, so they think all sorts of things: you're a spy in officer's uniform; you're a secret service man: you're a masquerading civilian; and I can't remember all the other things."

"Good Heavens," I said.

"My word, they're a lot of nitty-natterers!" cried George.

"What's more," added Dora, "they qualify what they say by pointing out you arrived here at the time it all started."

"Good Heavens," 'I repeated.

"By Jove," exclaimed George.

Later that evening I suggested we should take Mrs. Cranford with us when we made our enquiries, for we had two quite simple 'cases' to tackle: there was Mr. Ramon – whose presence in the tower was still a mystery, and Mr. Samson, who, having a dubious alibi on the night of the burglary, we were going to try to bluff into some sort of an admission. We should have to search for these men, approach them, and engage them in pleasant conversation; it would need the feminine touch, I thought. We decided to go first to the Blaydon Hotel, where we were bound to find discover Ramon, a habitual patron of Mrs. Dod's; then Samson might be found, we thought, at the Ship – anyway, we were prepared to hunt for him.

Arrived at the Blaydon after supper, we made a great clamour of conversation in the entrance hall, the copper bell clanging violently above all. Mrs. Dod welcomed us, and was about to take us upstairs to the lounge, when George said, "Ah – Mrs. Dod."

He beckoned to her with his finger. She laughed, coyly catching hold of his arm. In a hushed voice George gasped, "We

Tuesday

are on the trail – ah, Mrs. Dod. First, we shall quaff together – my wife! – and Peter! Here – eh – with – the proletariat – in the bar by the fire."

We all laughed; and it seemed to me that Mrs. Dod appeared a little apprehensive – but maybe that was my imagination. However, we crowded into the Public Bar, where Mr Ramon's husky form dominated the room, nearly reached the ceiling, and prevented the bar from falling outwards. He greeted me jovially, and I bought a round of drinks for Ramon and ourselves, while George pulled up chairs nearer to the fire for Dora's convenience. Dora was very quiet; she was watching. I sat next to her, Ramon next to me, and George nearest to the bar.

Ramon: "Well, here's health, Peter!"

George: "Wait – we must have – a toast –"

Peter: "What kind?"

George: "A toast to our friend here – Mr. Ramon."

Ramon: "What's that for? Why?"

George: "We must toast – I am glad to say – to your lucky escape – from danger the other day."

Ramon: "Thank you, Mr. Cranford. It was a nasty business that. And I must thank you, Peter, for trying to help me when I was first taken."

Peter: "To Mr. Ramon – prosperity and success."

Dora: "Yes, to Mr. Ramon."

Ramon: "That's very kind of you, I'm sure."

George: "What happened to you? That must have been very humiliating for you?"

Ramon: "Yes it was. Listen, I'll tell you all confidentially,

The Letters

because I know I can trust you."

Peter: "We shan't repeat a thing you say."

Dora: "Of course we won't, Mr. Ramon."

Ramon: "I told the police a different story to the one I'm going to tell you because they would have twisted mine against me. I know old Stott for what he is."

George: "What did you tell them?"

Ramon: "Just that I went up there out of a morbid curiosity to see what I could see or find."

Peter: "That was clever. Did they question you any further?"

Ramon: "Oh yes, but I wasn't saying anything. I just stuck to that story and nothing else."

George: "And what was the real story?"

Ramon: "Am I speaking too low for you to hear, Mrs. Cranford?"

Dora: "No, Mr. Ramon – I can hear. This is very exciting."

Ramon: "I've been suspicious of poor old Griefly. He was quite a friend of mine. Used to drink together at times. He's been different recently."

Peter: "But isn't that natural? – I mean Jane and all that."

Ramon: "Yes – but he was different before that!"

George: "How do you mean 'different'?"

Ramon: "Well, he seemed to act strangely. Looked worried. Didn't talk much – and he was usually a great talker, was old Griefly."

Peter: "Excuse me butting in so often, but – have you seen

Tuesday

this morning's local paper?"

Ramon: "No. Can't say I have. Bit busy you know."

Peter: "You must read it. They've published a letter left by Griefly, written immediately before his death."

George: "Yes, yes – but that can come later. Mr. Ramon's telling his story –"

Peter: "I'm sorry Mr. Ramon."

Ramon: "That's all right, Peter. I should be very interested to read that letter, but at the moment I must get on with my party-piece!"

Dora: "Yes?"

Ramon: "I was walking down the street on the Sunday when I saw Griefly go into the church. 'Hullo,' I thought. 'That's funny, he doesn't usually go to Church.' I seemed to link together in my mind my suspicions, and him being worried, and everything. So I thought I'd follow him, see what he was up to and stop him if he did anything silly. I couldn't see him in the church, and it was some time before I thought of the steeple. I started to climb the stairs – the door at the bottom had been broken open."

Peter: "Really?"

Ramon: "Yes. But when I was nearly at the top, I heard a horrible thud and a scream, and shouts. I was too late. I went up and cautiously looked down from behind a buttress, and saw him dead. I knew I was in a bad position myself so I sat beside the steeple, hiding. I was going to wait for an opportunity to escape. I heard you arrive on the scene, and I heard the ambulance go. I stood up, thinking I was doing it carefully – ready to go down. Then somebody saw me, and I was trapped."

George: "You were lucky, man. I'm glad."

Ramon: "Will you all have another drink – with me this time?"

Dora: "No thank you, Mr. Ramon. We've got to see some friends upstairs, and I rather think we're late already listening to your lovely story."

Peter: "Yes, we are a bit late, but it's been worth it."

George: "Yes, by Jove, that's a grand story, Ramon. Thanks for telling us."

Ramon: "Oh that's all right, but won't you stay for another drink?"

We assured him we could not, and George explained that we had only come in in the first place to get warm, for this was the snuggest room in the house.

Ramon was pleased, doubtless relieved to get a weight off his chest; George and I were pleased; and Mrs. Cranford was excited, though possibly a little shocked at her husband's unhesitating hypocrisy in his attitude toward Ramon, whom he disliked. She began to realise how much this investigation meant to George and me; and I think she was impressed.

We said 'good-night' to Ramon. George ordered him another beer.

Outside, George became the man of action, quite startling poor Dora who had seldom seen him behave like this before. His stick dangling from the crook of one arm, his great-coat thrown over his shoulder, his hat held high above his head in the other hand, he said, "Now – for the other! – er – this way, Dora!" He pushed Mrs. Cranford towards the door of the room beneath the stairs.

Was it George's incredible instinct or was it just chance that we should find there Master Samson himself? Later, George confessed that he had seen Samson pass the bar doorway. However, at the time we were very surprised: Mr.Samson sat

Tuesday

sprawled luxuriously across the wooden sofa. Opposite him was another youth more burly, more confident but younger. As we entered, Samson moved up to allow Mrs. Cranford room to sit next to him.

What would evolve from this next incident? I wondered how the bluff would come off, how George would put it over, what the outcome be. George was irrepressible that night; he went straight into the attack. I think his wife's presence had something to do with it, but whatever the motive he certainly was getting information.

"Good-evening, Samson – I see your glass is low. Won't you have another drink?" George began.

Samson wriggled and said, "Thank you, Sir."

"And your friend too – what'll you both have, eh?" As he said this, George pressed the bell.

Mrs. Dod's maid answered; and we soon had the frothing ale and the coloured gin before us on the glass top of the basket-work table.

George masterfully controlled the conversation, making it trickle like a stream meandering across the countryside, touching the Cinema, the News, the oratory of Churchill. Mrs. Cranford and I added our say, but we exchanged puzzled glances. Why was George doing this? Was he putting the fellow off his guard? When would he come to the point?

From some quite irrelevant subject George said sharply – and for no apparent reason –" Samson! We saw you at about one to half past – on Monday morning – early – round about the time of the burglary!" George was bluffing? We'd been in bed at that time.

The burly youth looked quite frightened. Samson was even more concerned. The suddenness of the question completely surprised him; he surrendered as unexpectedly and quickly as a Libyan strong point held by Italians when attacked at dawn with the bayonet. George's strategy had won.

"I was coming back from Hentham – from a dance," Samson said quickly. "The police know that – I told them."

George was determined. "Were you?" he said. "Then the police didn't get to know everything, did they?"

"I don't know what you mean," answered Samson, startled.

"Come, man! I've told you – we saw you that night – if you don't explain yourself, I shall make an immediate report to the police." George was convincing. Samson was defeated.

"I didn't mean to do it," he pleaded. "It was just a bit of fun. Wasn't it, Alf?" he asked his friend.

The burly youth, pale-faced, nodded his head in reply.

"You see, it was a bet," continued Samson, his voice faltering. "We had seen the motorbike put in that garage night after night. We knew the door there was never locked."

'"Motorbike" – "door never locked" – What did this mean?' I wondered.

The burly youth addressed as Alf seemed a very pleasant boy, quite different to Samson. He came to his friend's assistance at once.

"Yes, that's right, it was really my fault, I suppose," he said. "You see, I suggested Delil – I mean – Samson here should take it last Sunday night. Take the motorbike, that is. I sort of bet him a pound he wouldn't dare take it."

"That's right," agreed Samson, "and I won the bet. You see there wasn't any other way of getting to the dance – and I don't often get a chance of seeing my girl-friend Molly. Mother said I couldn't stay the night in Hentham, so there you are. That's how it happened."

Tuesday

"George," said Dora suddenly, "we must he going. We said we'd see the Thompsons, don't you remember?" We had not arranged any such meeting; Dora's sweet nature would no longer stand this shameful drama.

George looked sternly at Samson, who politely got to his feet as Dora stood up. "We'll say nothing. But take my advice, and don't mess about with military property. It's dangerous these days," he said.

I smiled, "Yes honestly, I don't think you quite understand the trouble to which you exposed yourself. We'll not tell the police, but we'll have to warn the Army authorities against it happening again."

Samson was nervously grateful, and Alf thanked us for being "awfully decent". George had bluffed perfectly, but had not obtained quite the information he expected; the interview seemed to indicate that we had one suspect less.

We said good-night to Mrs. Dod. When we had stepped into the blacked-out street, Mrs. Cranford said, "They're very young. You've got nothing there, George."

"No, but we've got a negative answer anyway. It cuts down the possible people. If only I could get the missing link – if only –" said George.

"Let's call at the Ship," I suggested. "We may find one of the Tank officers there – in fact, I think we're bound to. We could check up on the motorbike story then."

At Mrs. Black's we found Beryl and Capt. Ebbse having a drink together. Greetings over, we asked the Captain about the motorbike, and learnt that one of the battalion D.Rs. kept one in the hotel's court-yard garage. George told Ebbse in confidence what we had just heard from Samson. Ebbse was highly indignant. "Damned civilians" was his remark. I quietly pointed out that perhaps the Army was to blame in that the garage door had been unlocked – lack of security-mindedness. We parted, in consequence, as enemies.

Walking back to No.5, I said, "Well, what next? It looks like a dead-lock to me. Where's the missing link? Who is it? Why?"

Dora said, "I've got a queer feeling it's coming to an end. I don't know why, but it's just one of those female intuitions. You know what I mean, Peter? It's funny, isn't it?"

I agreed that it was funny: George thought it was not.

"Look," I said. "We've only got a few names left. After all, there's only Samson, who's too darned soft to hurt anybody – look how scared he was tonight –"

"He might have been acting," interrupted George.

"Mm? Then there's Ramon. He seems to explain himself pretty well – and anyway, he's got no motive. There's Mrs. Dod, and can you think of anything so absurd? She was at the Blaydon serving beer at the time of the murder."

"She might have been an accomplice," George pointed out.

"Oh George!" said Dora, as we walked over the level-crossing.

"There's Baker, a rough type whose only wrong has been to resent our questioning him."

"Peter, that's where you're wrong," said George. "He it is who has a motive – and local knowledge – and physical strength."

"But," I remarked, "He's not been seen with Jane Griefly for a long time; you said so yourself. There's no motive there. If he was in love, he'd have been seen with her frequently, wouldn't he? It stands to reason, I mean."

"That's right, Peter," Dora agreed.

Tuesday

We entered No. 5; took off our coats; and while George and I sat down by the fire, Dora bustled out into the kitchenette to make some tea.

"What about Edwards?" I asked, "He's been darned suspicious the whole way through, though I do think his chief worry has been that of prejudicing his military career should he be involved with the civil police."

George smiled, "I think you're right there – so who is it? There aren't any others of importance, are there?"

"Only Mr. Bromley," I laughed. "He was quite like the advert for Sandeman's Port that first night on the train."

George said, "Yes. Well, who do you think is our man?"

"All things considered as per Gilbert Keith, I believe Baker – as you mentioned just now – is our man. He's a nasty piece of work, and fits in like the last piece of a jig-saw puzzle – well, not quite, but he seems the only possibility."

"Yes," murmured George to himself, "Yes, he does."

We talked and drank tea, and went to bed.

CHAPTER VI: GRENADE - WEDNESDAY

I was having my breakfast; Mrs. Cranford was rattling crockery in the kitchenette with alarming energy; and George was having a bath. Since George was in his bath, it is not surprising that he should suddenly have splashed to his feet shouting, "Eureka!" but neither Dora nor I were prepared for such an exclamation, made in the most strident tones: I heard the clatter of falling plates, as I choked violently, my tea having missed my oesophagus.

"Eureka!" shouted George.

Dora rushed into the sitting room, her cheeks blushing, fearful that her husband would imitate the conclusion of the legend relating to his cry; he did not. In fact, it was not until half an hour had passed away, and George was seated ready for his food, that we had any intimation of his meaning.

"Dora, I am going to Newcastle by the 10.30 – business. I shall be back for tea, I expect – round about five or six. Excuse me – Peter – er, won't you?" he declared.

Mrs. Cranford laughed, "Oh Peter! Yes – I expect he's going there to make the big arrest."

George did not think it was funny; he said, "You must take this seriously Dore. This morning's work – ah – has nothing to do with – er – the matter – although, I will say that it might have." With this enlightening remark, he attacked the amoeba white of his two fried eggs, causing the bulbous yellow centre to burst and spread across the plate; it seemed that George had pricked the mystery, and the answer flowed out easily.

I wondered why he was going to Newcastle: was it just 'on business', or was there something else?

I remembered that I had very little money left. "I say, Mrs.

Wednesday

Cranford, do you mind if I slip into Hentham this morning, only I'd like to go to the bank, and do one or two oddments there. I'd be back for lunch."

"That's quite all right, Peter. I've quite a lot to do here this morning," she replied.

"Oh, so you want me out of the way, eh?" I asked laughing.

"Yes, of course, Peter. Look, you know, you could go in with George, couldn't you?" she suggested.

George and I caught the 10.30. We sat sleepily breathing the tobacco atmosphere, and stamping our feet to keep them warm. Neither of us had much to say, and Hentham soon loomed out of the fog, which still hung round the outskirts. I stood up to go.

"You know, Peter," said George solemnly, "it all depends on letters, man – I'm sure that letters are our answer – as indeed I've said before."

"Letters?" I asked, puzzled, and not very sure what he was talking about, "What kind of letters?"

"Letters you write –" he replied cryptically.

It was at the bank in Hentham that there occurred the incident which, so trivial and so nearly forgotten, eventually proved a major point in the tracking down of our man. Leaning on the counter, I was about to engage the attention of one of the idle clerks, when a voice called, "Well m'boy, how are you finding Halt Bridge? What did I tell you? It's a queer do all right, isn't it?"

I seemed to recognise the voice, but could not associate it with anybody I knew, so I turned round to see the fat lines, and scarlet face of the merry Mr. Bromley, whom I had met on the train that first evening. It seemed an age since that time, so after greeting him with relative fervour, I mentioned the fact.

"Yes," he said. "What a lot's happened, hasn't it? You didn't expect all that, did you? You mark my words, there's plenty done, and plenty doing. You see it's like this. I'm not dumb, and I've got ideas. Now I've been watching. Carefully." He paused to wipe a dirty blotch from his nose, a blotch which had been making him squint unconsciously as he spoke. I nodded my head, smiling encouragement. Mr. Bromley went on, "I've got my suspicions same as everybody else, but I think what nobody else thinks, and it's because what I think is logic – see what I mean?"

I did not quite see what he meant, but I said, "How interesting! and what do you think?"

"What do I think?" queried Bromley with wide open eyes and a sergeant-major wink. "Listen. Now don't tell anybody like, because I don't want to cause any trouble, see? But what about that fellow Baker, I say? What about him?"

I quietly asked, "What about him?"

"Well," said Mr. Bromley with a deep-throated snort. "Look at the burglary. Look at the thief's escape – bloke must've known the river pretty well. Gets deep in parts, y'know."

"True," I agreed, "I've waded there myself – saw a Corporal try it one night for a bet – when he was drunk. So I know how treacherous it is!"

"Yes, a bloke who's lived here as long as him ought to know it. He's also been a lover of that Jane. I know – most people have forgotten."

(I made a mental note on George's remarkable mind, that it should have been both so observant and retentive on the subject of Jane – a nothing girl in his life, in a place he visited infrequently.)

"And why," asked Mr. Bromley, "should he want to do this? Why, I ask?" He stared silently at me. Impressively he played his trump card. "Blackmail!" he said hoarsely. "Blackmail, that's what it is! He made her pregnant, and she tried to blackmail him, so he did

Wednesday

away with her. Did it cleverly, mind. Made it look like Cummings did it. Must have waited his opportunity."

I was amazed to hear this theory, which George and I had never even contemplated. It was good, and fitted in perfectly. Perhaps he was right – then all we had to do was work on Baker – anyway, we had our strongest suspicions on him already. George would like to know this.

As suddenly as a momentary splash of water from the tap of a Cairo hotel bath-room, two Hentham clerks wakened, yawned, and approached us. What could they do for us? I was no longer impatiently belligerent, but rather jubilant at what appeared to be a new discovery; if only I had realised that the real discovery was yet to come!

No. 1 Clerk said, "Yes, sir."

No. 2 Clerk said, "Morning, sir."

I explained what I required, and No. 2 slouched away.

Mr. Bromley said, "Putting in my savings for the kids after the war same as usual."

No.1 said, "Just a moment, Sir. I'll get you the certificates."

Mr.Bromley and I, left to ourselves again, discussed Savings and the war.

No.2 returned. "Here, sir. Fill this up here," he said brusquely.

"Where?" I asked.

"Along the line at the bottom of course, sir," said No. 2 pityingly.

I was about to open an argument as to which line should bear my signature, when No. 1 returned with some certificate forms

The Letters

for Mr. Bromley. "This is what you want, sir," he exclaimed.

Mr. Bromley replied, "Thanks – but have you got five pounds worth there? It doesn't look much like it."

"I'm sorry, sir. Why didn't you tell me in the first place? You don't usually want as much as that. You generally get two quids' worth a week only," No. 1 answered quickly. Mr. Bromley became rudely angry, and No. 1 retired sulkily upon his second errand, his suede shoes squelching on the tiled floor behind the counter.

Presently I received my money from the begrudging hands of No. 2, and biding Mr. Bromley a hurried adieu, I left him to ravage the lethargy of both the clerks. As I walked into the crisp Hentham air, I had no other thought than morning coffee at the Crown Hotel!

Arriving at No. 5 in time for lunch, I was delighted to find Mrs. Cranford waving a telegram to me from her bedroom window. The cable was from home. My Mother said simply: "Arriving Thursday about six stop."

Dora was still as curious as I concerning George's sudden business appointment, because he had made no previous mention of it, nor had he received any mail during the week, so we believed he must have gone to Newcastle to make enquiries about the Griefly case. We wondered if this were so, where he could indeed have found out anything there; but no satisfactory answer evolved from our conversation.

The afternoon dragged past. Dora and I went for a walk to quell our impatience, but it was only four 'clock, when we returned for tea; and it was another two hours before George actually arrived. He appeared, as he tapped his way down the path with his stick, to be in a great state of excitement. He greeted his wife with a kiss; and myself with these words: "Ay man – I have some information – er – of considerable import."

"What is it? Come on in and tell us," I asked eagerly.

Wednesday

"Come on in, George, and have some tea," suggested Dora.

"By Jove – I shall need more than that, Dora. We must have our supper early, for there is work to be done!" Then turning to me: "Something is afoot, Peter. We're on the trail in real style. But we must put our heads together first. There is still a missing link."

We jostled into the sitting room, Dora helping George to take off his coat. The fire crackled and snapped in the grate; the yellow flames lighted the darkening room; and George the unromantic, George the realist once more broke a spell by pressing the light switch.

Mrs. Cranford had fixed the preliminaries for our meal; George had drunk his tea; and I had withheld my question till this moment.

"What have you to tell us?" I asked suddenly.

Mrs. Cranford felt as I did, for she instantly supported me, saying, "Yes, George what've you been doing? Where've you been?"

He was the centre of attraction; he ruled the scene; he said: "Who said I'd been anywhere?"

It was five minutes later that George really began to give us some idea of his Newcastle programme. Apparently his 'vision' had struck him – after long thought on the previous night – simultaneously with his accidentally turning on the cold instead of the hot tap, whilst he was seated in his bath.

"It came to me so suddenly that I might have been standing before Damascus," said George. There ensued a long explanation showing the relativity of St. Paul's vision and his own inspiration; it was Dora who recalled him to the business in hand.

"But what was it, George?"

"My dear, it was Cummings."

The Letters

"What do you mean?" I asked, startled, "Not that Cummings did it?"

"No, no, of course not, no," George rebuked. "I mean that Cummings was the man to question. Remember, the police would not accept his statement, so that no information about what he said to them reached the public – or us, eh?"

Dora and I gasped and whistled respectively, both in admiration for the Great Man's far-seeing intelligence and imagination.

"Now don't interrupt," our hero remonstrated again. "I shall tell you my tale as briefly as I can."

"Oh, just a moment, George," cried Dora. "The potatoes are boiling over."

With similar obstacles, with numerous irrelevant similes, illustrative stories, and philosophical observations, George struggled through the events of his day. He thought Cummings might have some 'data', so he went up to see him; he was able to speak to the lieutenant with surprising ease, though his conversation was attended by two constables; and he was told the prisoner's story in full when he explained the significance of his mission.

"I will try to tell in words as near to Cummings' – as I am able, the story as far as – he is concerned," George began. And he spoke remarkably briefly with very few diversions, with very little explanation, and with quite incredible simplicity.

"'My brother ' – That's to say Cummings' brother, the boy, whom Griefly murdered," George pointed out. "'My brother wrote and told me about a girl with whom he had fallen in love. Somehow my brother read a letter of hers which showed that the girl was carrying on a basely illicit and secret love-affair. Now you know most of the rest – apparently the girl became pregnant, and was going to make a dastardly accusation against my brother. I'm told

Wednesday

Griefly intercepted a letter from Jane to my brother, and the result was the death of all three of them.' I asked Cummings then what he had himself had to do with the girl. He said, 'I thought after my special knowledge that there was something fishy in this police "accident" theory, so I went down to investigate. I put up at the Dutch House. I soon found Jane in the village – with her bright red hair, described to me by my brother. I identified her type. Donning my uniform late that afternoon, I naturally, as it were, soon vamped the girl, for so long as a man was an officer he was O.K. by Jane. We decided to go for a walk, or rather she did, so we went down the Sidley road, as it was getting dark. I had intended later giving her a good talking to, thinking she had been the cause of my brother's suicide. We spoke of my brother when we had gone some way out of Halt Bridge. At last she pulled me by the arm down a side turning. It was Sidley Bridge. Her heartlessness, her abandon, and her coy minxishness made me very angry. I lost my temper, ticked her off violently, and turned about, leaving her there alone. After I'd gone about a hundred yards I pulled myself together, remembering my manners enough to know I should have to escort her back through the dark. I returned and saw a black shape, which began to run away towards Sidley Hall. I could hear the clump of heavy boots.

"'I thought the wretched girl had fooled me, bringing me out to Sidley, where she anyway intended leaving me, already having arranged to meet somebody else there. I imagined her and the man running into the night, laughing at me. Very annoyed, I made my way back to my hotel thinking I had made a fool of myself and had wasted my time. The next morning I left by the first train. Later that day I was arrested for the girl's murder. Nobody was more surprised than I.'"

I asked what the police had done, if they had been at all reasonable with his story.

"No, the police," said George, "were quite sure that Cummings was guilty. 'It was,' they declared, 'too obvious.' And you will agree his story is a little frail, isn't it?"

"Yes, it is. Well, well, so that's how things are! Well done. But how does that affect us? an illicit love-affair, pregnancy –"

"What are you murmuring about, Peter? eh, man?"

"Blackmail!" I shouted. "Blackmail, that's it. Or it could be. I'll tell you. Oh Christmas! This is terrific. I may have got it all now. Oh what a day!"

George and Dora looked at each other puzzled.

More calmly I said, "Let me tell you what my experiences were in Hentham this morning. Nothing dramatic at all. But – I wonder –" I explained briefly the incident at the bank. George after a short pause said, "But what, man – has this got to do with us? eh?" He laughed kindly, and as though to make up for his reception of my experience added, "I must say, though, old Bromley's served us up with a pretty theory. What say you – er – Dora?"

Before Dora could say what she thought, I explained, "This chap Bromley gave me a theory, didn't he? said he believed Baker was the man? said it all so – as it were – nonchalantly, didn't he? That's one point. Was he suggesting something to me? did he realise you and I were 'on the trail'? You see I'm pretty well working this out as I go along, because the thing's only just come to me. Anyway, number two point is most important, and number one just qualifies it. Isn't it significant that Bromley should be putting in another three pounds more than usual?"

"Why?" asked George bluntly.

"Because – well, let's suppose he's X, shall we?"

"Good Heavens, man!"

"Please listen. Supposing he's X. Jane Griefly's dead. He no longer has to pay her her money – possibly weekly – as blackmail! He now can pay that extra into his savings for his children. And another thing – who is more in a position for blackmail, and for

Page 94   Next Chapter starts on Page 109

Wednesday

committing murder on this account than a married, respectable man with several children, a man who's lived in Halt Bridge so long?"

There was a long silence. George stood to his feet suddenly, knocking over a vase containing the corpse of some plant.

"George, you really are careless," Dora scolded. This was going to be a dramatic moment, but it had been spoiled now; however, George, looking a little hurt and ignoring his wife's rebuke, also the irreparable damage to the pot with the corpse, extended his arm theatrically.

"Petah, man – you're right. I believe – yes – I believe – that our young friend – ah – is right. And now – I have an announcement to make to you both."

"What a mess!" said Dora sweeping up the corpse's debris from around George's feet.

"Dore!" said George indignantly. "What is this? – I am speaking. – I have had a trump card up my sleeve for some time. You may – ah – recall, I mentioned it – only yesterday. I thought of a method of trapping the murderer! – Even if – we did not have enough proof to convict him!"

"What!" Dora and I cried together.

"Remember I said to you, as you left the train this morning 'It all depends on letters' -? It does. Letters are the key to this case. Bluff is the key of life. Eh? What say you, man?"

There was a long pause. I listened to the crackling of the fire. I looked at George standing there with his eyes half closed, staring at a hole in the carpet.

"Letters? Bluff? Please explain?" I asked.

"I have it. We must act – to-night. Listen, this was my idea – to trick the murderer into confession by bluff – suppose we had a bundle of letters – suppose we said they were letters overlooked at

The Letters

Mrs. Griefly's place – suppose, man, we suggested they had something incriminating in them – might even hint an illicit lover –"

"George," I interrupted with unusual familiarity, "that's great. We can go out, find Bromley – we can get him a drink, talk to him, bring the subject round, and at the critical moment produce the phoney packet."

"Phoney packet?" queried George. "What is that, man?"

Dora laughed, "The bluff packet of letters of course."

"You're terrific. What a party! Are you coming too, Mrs. Cranford?"

"No," answered George. "Dore, you go to the Thompsons. We shall join you there later. You must not be there to-night. It might not be safe."

In this simple way our plans were made: to find Bromley, to drink with him, to discuss the murders, to show the course of our investigations, to try out the trick, and to hope for the best. It was dangerous but we hoped it would be worth the risks; we were, as Mrs. Cranford pointed out, "putting all our eggs in one basket", for so much depended on our success, so much could go wrong. If Bromley was not the murderer, he might even file a libel action against us; and if he was the murderer, he might not be tricked, might indeed get us into trouble, and would certainly be on his guard against us in the future. We were taking risks, but in life chance plays a hand with bluff; and an innocent man's life depended on our effort.

As George was tying up a neat pile of envelopes which I had been marking, Dora suddenly took the leading role of our drama.

"George, I don't want to criticise. I only want to make a suggestion."

"Yes," said George, interested.

Wednesday

"Is it wise to have a packet of letters? Wouldn't it be better to have, say, one or two?"

I asked why.

She said, "If you have a bundle, he may have sufficient memory of the number of letters he's written to Jane. One or two he might easily imagine he's mislaid, but not a whole bundle!"

"Dora, why didn't you tell us before, and save us wasting our time on these dummies?"

"George! is that all the gratitude – ?"

The domestic situation eased. Dora was rightfully lauded, and we altered our plans accordingly. There would be three letters only, letters whose origin we should decide later – whether they were from perhaps Jane to somebody else asking advice, whether they were from Bromley himself to her hinting the situation, or whether they were a mixture of the two.

We ate our meal, dressed ourselves, and all three walked out into the fresh, cold, night air. What could the night bring? success or failure? We all three must have wondered as we passed the level crossing. I remarked on the gates being open for the first time in George's history, intimating that this was a good omen. At the Station Hotel we parted, Dora to go to the Cottage and wait with the Thompsons, George and I to take our first step in the most exciting, most dangerous part of our adventure. The Church clock struck a quarter to eight as we entered the pub.

We stayed for ten minutes or so drinking half a pint of ale each, and talking to Ernie, who told us that Bromley was not in any of the bars. Saying good-night, we left, crossing the bridge to the Ship.

It was just after eight, when we sat down by a table near the fire-place to take our quaff. George was in great humour, though I must admit to being a little apprehensive about the proposed affair.

The Letters

Bromley was not in the lounge, and a quick reconnaissance of the public bar showed that he was not there either. We decided to wait a little while, as we had done at the Ernies. Should Bromley appear, my job – on the grounds that I was acquainted with him – was to ask him to sit and have a drink with us.

Bromley seemed fated to enter the Ship some five or ten minutes after us. I felt my cheeks burning beneath their outer tan, as I stood to my feet in a dream, attracted his attention to our table, and ordered his drink. Looking at George's face I gained confidence, for there was in his keen eyes a stern, yet humorous, care-free light, which inspired, and at the same time completed the unreality of the scene: a table, drinks, a saloon bar, a fire, talking people, and a game of wits, playing with life itself, was about to begin; the whole idea drugged me so much that I wondered if I should be able to say my part when the time came. I was recalled from my reverie by George's reassuring voice.

"Peter here has been telling me of a remarkable theory of yours, Bromley," he was saying.

Bromley lifted a fat eye-brow. The idea of Mr. Bromley being a murderer seemed ridiculous. I stared at the man, then forced myself to grin sheepishly at him.

George continued, "A theory about the murder business – you suggest blackmail, and I agree with you – entirely."

"Thanks, Mr. Cranford," said Bromley lifting his glass. "Your very good health."

George was persistent. "I have a theory too, Mr. Bromley, a theory of letters."

I thought I saw Bromley clutch his glass more tightly.

"But before I tell you about it, let me explain something about ourselves in connection – er – with the past few days."

Wednesday

Bromley had a puzzled expression on his face. "Why certainly. I'd like to listen. I've heard you were both on holiday. Hope you've enjoyed yourselves." The man was clever. I again wondered if we were not about to make ourselves look very foolish, but my heart beat faster.

"Right," said George. "We thought we'd look into this – matter. You see we were convinced the naval Officer was innocent."

"Very true," said Bromley nodding his head and wagging his finger simultaneously. "He had nothing to do with it – and as I was saying to Peter this morning –" He broke off to look over his shoulder, then went on in a hushed voice, "As I said, it's that Baker bloke every time. Everything goes to prove it."

George said, "We thought that – at first."

"What?" gasped Bromley, with what I imagined to be mock surprise. "You think there's somebody else?"

"Yes, I have proof of it," George remarked placidly. "Listen. First let's take Cummings' case – he did not do it. His position was far too obvious. Look how he was found lunching at the Turk's Head! Ridiculous, eh?"

Bromley and I nodded. Bromley asked where the letters came into it. George, who had begun to wander in his conversation, returned to the issue. "Ah yes. The letters – I must tell you a tale – er – of letters – as you will see – But recall to mind the events. There was a letter from Jane to Cummings junior, eh? Intercepted by Griefly, it was altered and despatched – fatally."

Bromley was lounging back in his chair, his glass in his hand resting on the chair arm; I wondered if this was to put himself at ease. His paunch stirred uneasily beneath his bulging waist-coat. George was staring sternly at him. The man, who modelled his powerful character on his idol the Prime Minister, spoke again. "One letter discovered by Cummings junior showed that there was an illicit love-affair in Jane's life. Queer, wasn't it? Then there were

The Letters

those important letters stolen from the Grieflys' house – ah – Unexpectedly, there followed the letter left by Griefly, giving reasons for his death. And there are other letters besides."

"What letters are they?" enquired Bromley quietly.

"Not yet, not yet," said George glibly, as though he were rehearsing the act with me at No. 5. How exceptionally well he steered his course!

It was my turn to speak, for George had nodded his head in my direction. "We suspected a number of people," I said, adding quickly to allay any suspicions, which he might be harbouring. "This is of course very confidential, you know."

Mr. Bromley said nothing; his eyes narrowed; and he nodded his head up and down very slowly, so that the wrinkles of fat on his neck rolled and unrolled like carpets beaten and for beating. I explained to him carefully the result of our investigation: "We believed Jane had definitely been murdered, for so heartless and level-headed a girl would have died by neither suicide nor accident that night on the bridge: that Mr. Griefly was the culprit was out of the question, for even supposing him to be mad, and to have committed the murder, he would most certainly have mentioned the fact in his last letter: that Lt. Edwards of the local Tank unit was innocent, because he did not know the course of the Tyne, and we believed the burglar of the letters and the murderer to be well acquainted with the village: Mrs. Dod –"

"Not so fast, Peter man," George interrupted. "Mr. Bromley doesn't understand. You see, Bromley, all these people whom Peter is naming were once on our suspect list – for one reason or another."

Bromley made no comment, so I started again where I had left off. "Mrs. Dod we had hardly considered, since everybody knew she was serving in her hotel at the time of the deed: Mr. Samson we thought was a foolish boy who had very nearly got himself into serious trouble, but his alibi was accurate, for we had seen him in

Wednesday

the pub on the eventful night: and there was Mr. Ramon, whose sympathetic attentions to Mrs. Griefly we accepted as being sincere; he had no reason to kill Jane."

When I had finished talking, I stood up to attract Mrs. Black's attention. "More beer all round please, Mrs. Black," I asked.

Mr. Bromley beamed his admiration. "You've been going it all right," he acknowledged. "My goodness! I have done some thinking too – and some original thinking, but I didn't go so far afield as that. Still I didn't have the time of you gentlemen. I just watched and thought about it. I noticed you haven't mentioned two things."

"And er – what are they, Bromley – may I ask?" inquired George.

"You've not said who did do the murder, and you've not mentioned Baker."

He launched himself into a sitting position in his chair, placed his empty glass on the table, and looking at George said: "And Baker's the man! But have your investigations found any proof? Have they? When's the coup coming off?"

'Was there a sneer in that last question?' I wondered. 'What was he thinking about? Did he feel concerned? Could he really be the murderer? What was going to happen next?' The next event was the second issue of drinks, for which I dreamily paid.

George took the stage: "Now, Baker was our man. Everything pointed to it."

"Was? Pointed?" repeated Bromley, accentuating the past tense. "How do you mean?"

"That we no longer think so," replied George smiling. Bromley accepted this answer without question. He lifted his glass as though to change the subject, and said "Cheers!" He drank most of the beer in one gulp.

The Letters

"Baker was the only possible case. He had a motive, either the jealous lover, or the blackmail motive, which you gave to us. He knew Halt Bridge – like the back of his hand, so he would have known about the river. He was surly, when tackled on the question of Jane. But he did not kill Jane Griefly." George's voice trembled as he spoke the last words; I knew the climax was near, and I drank a long draught of ale. I watched Bromley's face, which had set like a marble bust; his eyes glinted with a strange light; he remained leaning forwards, quite still. He had changed, no longer the merry Falstaff, now the anxious Faustus. I knew we were right, but should we succeed?

George went on, "Another person, whom we've only just discovered – did the murder, a dirty, foul murder, Mr. Bromley."

Bromley stared back at George, but his appearance never altered; he was like a statue, a marble toad, only his wicked eyes glinted.

"Do you recall these words?" I asked: "'There's no good in the air. Just you see.' You should. Don't you remember when I arrived last Friday evening? – in the train?"

Bromley still stared at George.

"Those were your words – an accurate forecast of things to come, wasn't it?" George paused, then in a nonchalant tone of voice said, "We'll call the murderer X, shall we? Eh? X blunders, tells us the key to the riddle. He – yes, it's a man, Mr. Bromley, a married man with children – gives us a clue at exactly the time – that we ourselves discover – a further point . We find out that this X is probably the illicit secret lover of Jane. Why should he be that? Perhaps it's because he's married – eh? Perhaps he caused the girl's pregnancy? Perhaps she blackmailed him? Perhaps that's why one week after the murder, X is able to put aside more money than usual – eh, Mr. Bromley? What say you?"

The man was about to speak when George dramatically withdrew the letters from his pocket, and said, "These letters I have

Wednesday

here – are conclusive proof – of our investigations. They are written by Jane Griefly to an old school friend of hers in Alston. This – ah – friend sent the letters on to Mrs. Griefly, who gave them to us. These letters explain the plight which Jane was in. They explain a number of other things." He paused, then said very slowly, "Jane writes the name of – her lover, the murderer."

There was a short silence.

George said quietly, "Mr. Bromley, you murdered Jane Griefly."

I thought for a moment Bromley would strike George. He gripped the arms of his chair tightly; he leaned further across the table, his stomach pressing hard against its outer rim; and he glared with such terrible rage that anyone but George Cranford must have quailed. George merely finished off his beer. None of us said a word. Presently Bromley sat back in his chair. He calmly ordered more beer.

Suddenly he caught hold of my hand. "You're right," he said, "but you won't get away with this. I've got something in my pocket which will blow everybody in this bar to Hell. I'm in the Home Guard, you know, and I've carried this little thing about with me for the past week – just in case. I shall use it, if you don't give me time to clear out of here, and get a good start. Now let's talk this over nice and quietly. Listen, I've got my family, my wife and children to think of …"

George said, "You should have thought of that before."

"And we've got to think of an innocent man, who would otherwise be going to his death – Cummings," I said aggressively.

Mr. Bromley half jeering, half pleading gave his reasons for his life against Cummings': "He's a Naval bloke. You know what they are, drinking, women – same type as the kid brother. He was single too. I've got my wife and kids. I've only made one mistake in my life, one weakness, a temptation. Then I was blackmailed. I had

The Letters

a night to kill the girl. She was rotten. Why must this happen?" His voice grew passionate and louder. His eyes became wild, wide-open. He gripped the table so that his knuckles were white; and he grasped my hand painfully. Those people nearest our table had stopped talking to listen to our conversation. Presently there was complete silence in the lounge. Everybody stared at us, as though expecting a scene. Bromley was overheard, trapped.

George said, "No, Bromley."

I was very angry. "Who the Devil are you to put up your life against another man's? You snivelling, despicable rat!" I cried.

George warned me to be "steady, man".

Trembling, Mr. Bromley began to rise to his feet. The moment had come. The slight flab of his cheeks appeared to quaver; his eyes never left George's face; there was hatred in them; and he looked of a sudden old and eaten up with the evil cancer which was now about to bring him to the grave. The past few minutes must have been a great strain on the man; he lost control of himself and panicked. Standing, he looked about the room, then edged his way backwards to a position commanding the door and at the same time the occupants of the lounge. Since a scene was unavoidable George rose to his feet, beaming upon his audience. "This man," he said, "murdered Jane Griefly."

There were gasps from the startled drinkers; one lady fainted; another stifled a scream with her hand; and there was quiet again. I was watching Bromley carefully, waiting for his next move; and wished I had brought my 'Mauser' with me.

An impetuous youth began to push his way noisily through the tables and chairs towards Mr. Bromley, who at once took something from his pocket. I heard the tinkle of metal against the glass surface of one of the tables, as he tossed a small object onto it. I realised with a pang of fear, recalling the desert days, what Mr. Bromley had done. The safety pin of a bomb had fallen with a clink. He was holding up for all to see a Mills 36 hand grenade.

Page 104   Next Chapter starts on Page 109

Wednesday

"Stand back there. Don't be a fool. You'll have us all killed!" George shouted to the young man, who stopped immediately.

It was a strange scene: men and women stood against the walls staring at the drama amidst the furniture in the centre of the floor. George and I were standing by our table. The young man was a little behind us. I noticed how the glasses winked, reflecting the orange of the jumping flames in the fireplace; a log broke apart and fell with a sharp bump into the grate: one notices these small things in times of stress or danger. Halt Bridge would remember this for years to come, since there was a number of the old stagers amongst the crowd.

Mr. Bromley said, "Stay where you are. I'm getting out of this door. If anybody attempts to follow me, I'll blow you all up. Give me a good start, or I'll throw this in the street, killing more innocent people, and neither you nor I want that. I did kill Jane Griefly, but I'm not sorry. These clever gents know why. On that Friday night I followed the couple out there – they didn't realise because it was too dark to see me." He added, "And these gents didn't know that."

He waved his hand towards us as he said this, and I saw my chance. Taking a quick, short, running jump I landed by Bromley. It was a surprise movement and I managed to grasp the grenade. Gripping it firmly so as to hold the lever down, I banged his wrist hard against the wall, and pulled the grenade away from him. At this very opportune moment Mrs. Black opened the door. Knocking her tray full of drinks all ever her, I dashed outside followed closely by Bromley, the impetuous youth, and George. As I ran out into the night, Bromley hit me viciously behind the ear, so that I stumbled, accidentally releasing the grenade lever. I promptly threw the grenade across the little garden, over the wall, and into the river, where it exploded harmlessly. I have never before heard a 36 make so much noise; they must have heard it in Haltwhistle.

Bromley just had time to hit me on the chin; and he knocked me down, so that I banged my head on the cobble stones. I saw the young man grip him round the neck with both hands, and kick him in the spine.

Mr. Bromley collapsed at the same time as I.

My wits returned to me, and I sat up. I was in Mrs. Black's sitting room; George was seated next to me. "Eh, man," he said. "That was risky. How are you feeling?"

"Wow! I got a three-way bump then. Who was the Errol Flynn?" I replied, rubbing my head and my ear and my chin all at the same time. "He did a very nice job on old fatty Bromley. What's happened since then?"

George smiled. "You've only been unconscious a few minutes, though we were a little – ah – worried, at first man. I've sent for Stott, and that's Bromley over there. He pointed to the other side of the room, where the fat man, his head upon a pillow, lolled upon the floor gasping. On a chair by his side sat an old man whom I recognised as one of the three whom we had seen on that first night at the Ship; dressed in Home Guard's uniform, he held a service rifle firmly across his knees. I laughed.

"And what about Mrs. Black?" I asked.

"She understood, when I explained to her, and immediately put her private room at our disposal," he answered, adding, "but she was very angry at first – broken glasses, drink all down her dress, thrown into a sitting position on the bottom stair! By Jove, man, enough to upset anybody, what?"

"But please tell me who was –"

George interrupted me, "Here's the man!"

The door opened; it was Alf, Samson's young friend.

"Hallo! That was damn good work just now," I said. "Let's go and have a drink on it. I'm O.K. now."

Before George could stop me, I had disappeared bar-wards,

Wednesday

closely followed by the other two.

Jane presently called us from our 'party' with information that the 'police' had arrived, so we filed excitedly back to Mrs. Black's sitting room, where we found P.C. Stott already 'on the job.'

"Good evening, Stott" smirked George. "Do you want any help, Stott eh? You don't look quite so clever now, do you?"

Stott seemed so humiliated that we ordered him some whiskey, which he drank gratefully – protesting at the same time that this was not his normal conduct when on duty. We briefly told him the facts, but he said we should have to accompany him to his home, which represented the police station.

It was nearly nine o'clock, when we reached Stott's house. We told him in detail all we knew; when we finished it was unfortunately closing time for the pubs. A call was put through to Newcastle by the Inspector, who arrived from Hentham in answer to Stott's frantic appeals: Cummings' immediate release was ordered and an invitation added for him to stay for a few days with the Cranfords.

Cummings was free; we had attained our object.

Before leaving, we looked at Bromley, who was lying handcuffed on a sofa; the Home Guardsman still impassively watched over him. The fat man's back was obviously causing him a lot of pain. We were a little embarrassed.

George said, "Well, Bromley, I've not come to gloat, but to show you how with the help of Peter here I won our very dangerous game. It was by chance rather than ingenuity, or clever investigation."

Bromley was a changed man. He didn't look up. He was too distressed.

"Here are the letters I showed you," George said pulling the

The Letters

blank sheets of paper from the prepared envelopes.

The look upon Bromley's face on seeing this will be imprinted on my memory always – indignation, a terrible futile anger, hatred, and desperation were all expressed.

The great man, who had proved such a match for his opponents on the playing fields of Commerce, had shown once again his brilliance – in the theatre of crime; he was triumphant, yet his sympathetic heart bled for the creature which Bromley was now. As we were about to leave, George turned, saying quietly, "Take my tip, man. Play your cards to the Judge as you did with us, and you'll get away with your life. If you're clever enough, you may get only a short sentence – I'm sure of it. Ah – Good-night, Bromley."

The man recognised the fighter, the sportsman, the culture of this miniature Voltaire; for he weakly answered, "Good-night."

I closed the door; and as we went into Stott's room, I could hear the sound of sobbing.

P.C. Stott sent us on our way with instructions to "drop in some time to-morrow morning", as there were some more forms still to be filled up "etseterar".

The astonishment and incredulity and excitement of the folks at the Cottage was indescribable. However, the party closed down early on the grounds that Mrs. Thompson had invited us to have a tremendous party on the following night "in celebration of the extraordinary and successful climax of local events", as George said.

On the way back to No. 5 (it was after eleven o'clock) Dora said she had a 'phone call to make, so she kept George fuming by the War Memorial for at least fifteen minutes. George declared that he could not understand who she would have to ring up at that time of night; and he received no satisfactory reply from Dora to his question.

CHAPTER VII: GEORGE TELLS THE TALE - THURSDAY

It was Thursday evening; it was dark; and the pubs were open. A chink of orange light shone from between closely drawn dark curtains across one of the tiny cottage windows, and stretched itself over the moving river's face. Sounds came from inside the building, sounds which indicated the most hilarious of convivial parties.

The inside displayed a frenzied scene of happy activity; all the guests had become very well acquainted with each other and had already sorted themselves out into groups of varying, chattering numbers. Two couples were dancing to the crackling blare of the pleasantly tuneless gramophone; one small feminine group with heads sentimentally cocked as they surveyed the youthful vigour of the dancers, was seated by the sparkling fire; and a third standing by the drinks table laughed uproariously, for George held the stage in this quarter.

A spirit of good-will, strongly reminiscent of Christmas-time, dominated the gay little room. Spick and span amidst the merrymakers, the furniture, the carpet, all stayed miraculously in its proper place. The pale yellow of the clean walls, the polished black of the mantel-piece and hearth, the orange lamp, the glass-paned doorway to the miniature lobby, the rifle slung by its trigger guard on a nail in one of the white-painted rafters, and the "Woodchoppers Ball" ringing above the general hum, all contributed towards the most riotously happy little room in all Northumberland.

The record ended; Beryl placed a new one on the platform, and Nat Gonella played his trumpet for our special benefit. This was the Thompson's Cottage. This was our "night of nights". With the change of record, the scene itself changed; the various groups intermingled, split, and set into a new pattern, like quicksilver on a marble table stirred by a careless finger. Nobody danced. Each one

The Letters

tried to speak faster than his or her neighbour, and at least each male of the party did this between long sips of ale.

Sitting secluded on the right of the fire-place in one of the cushioned, wood-framed armchairs was Jean Thompson, our charming hostess, beaming personality upon the delighted company; she apparently found it possible to listen at the same time to Lieutenant Cummings' life story, which that young man was fervently and confidentially telling her.

Opposite her were Dora and Mrs. Cadogan with their offspring sitting in their usual position on the floor; they looked conspicuously jubilant. (Dora, when she had kept us waiting outside the telephone kiosk, had sent a cable to Sheila and Wendy, recalling them instantly for the proposed celebrations.)

Near the windowed door, behind which "Ken" two years previously had introduced his famous "lift" act, stood Mrs. Dod with Cpl. Hayworth (an R.A.F. boy, whom we had not seen before during the week, since he had been on special duty; this by a pleasant coincidence was his first night off. He used to do a lot of fishing with Mr. Cranford), and the "man of the moment", our great leader, our beloved "George", who swaying gently, appeared to "be haranguing a thousand unseen troops" before battle.

Over by the "drinks" table stood and sat the fourth group with dear Beryl, wretched Ebbse, and our lovable Bart; their conversation led by Bart was centred on cabbages, which Bart intended growing in the minute Cottage garden later in the New Year.

It was inevitable on an occasion such as this that George should speak. However, to my great embarrassment having called for silence, and attention, the small powerful man asked me to give an account for the benefit of "our new – and most welcome – ah – guests." Acknowledging the facetious clapping with a facetious bow of my head, I sadly began my story:

"Well, there's a lot's happened, but I'm not sure where to

Thursday

start, or just how brief I can make this, without the thread being lost, but I'll do my best," I said. "It's all about letters – as Mr. Cranford pointed out to me yesterday morning, when we were nearing the end of our adventure. You see, a treacherous letter written by a treacherous girl fell into the hands of her father, who not possessed with the full facts caused either directly or indirectly the death of an innocent man, the death of his wicked daughter, his own death, and also the dastardly imprisonment of an innocent man. Actually our first discovery –"

George, interrupting: "I have a toast to make!"

Dora: "George! That was very rude of you."

Everyone laughed; and George solemnly apologised, but continued with his proposal undeterred. Relieved of my responsibility, I breathed deeply again. George proceeded to call a toast to Lieutenant Cummings, who had suffered so much in the last two weeks; with one accord we all rose to our feet with glasses raised, and drank to his future success and happiness.

Then George took the floor, once more calling for quiet and order. But we knew George, and I fear that silence was never restored any more that night – not even for George, though he tried hard enough. The great, the historic man stood gallantly there, his feet astride, his glass half empty in one hand, his other hand gesticulating to emphasise points of special note. He gave us of his greatest Churchillian oratory, and warmed the cockles of our sozzled hearts.

"Ah – my friends – or should I say – er – comrades?"

Loud cheers.

"We are here to-night – for a purpose – for celebrations!"

Rude whistle, and ribald laughter.

"Of a kind, which we all know, and for which – we must pass

The Letters

a vote – of thanks to Mrs. Thompson."

Burst of cheering, and clapping.

"Ah – we are here – to-night –"

Yes, we were there all that night, and nearly all the early hours of the next morning. It was a morning which brought to an icy, happy ending that gayly hectic, tragically fantastic week

And although the party gathered there was broken up and once again dispersed widely over the face of England, the spirits which went to make it were not just "ships which pass in the night"; for the Cottage, and all that it represented, remained a living, golden memory in the hearts of us all.

ABOUT THE AUTHOR

We used to go to Southwold in Suffolk, every August, for three weeks of Summer holidays. Happy times spent in the beach hut and playing by the sea. And over supper, our father – Peter Carpmael – would tell my brothers and me the next episode in that year's story, which would last the full length of the holiday.

He loved writing and despite living a very busy life, running The Blue Cross, a national animal welfare charity, he wrote at least five novels. When he retired from The Blue Cross, our mother was disappointed though not surprised to find that he was setting off on yet one more novel – 'Was There Ever Seen Such Villainy' – a story that harks back to memories of his own summer holidays in Cornwall.

We think that 'The Letters' was written at the end of World War Two, when he was recovering from his wounds received at Monte Casino. The copy we have was typed onto the back of sheets of telexed news reports.

The fairyland books – 'The Magic Chatty' and 'Upon The Other Side' – were written towards the end of the 1940s, when he had started working for Our Dumb Friends League, which would later become The Blue Cross, and had got married. Children's stories were clearly on his mind.

After that, we know of at least one other novel - a long thriller which he had second thoughts about and eventually burned. It would be lovely to be able to read that one now !

He was born in 1920 and died at 97 in 2018.

John Carpmael, 2021

Peter Carpmael in military uniform

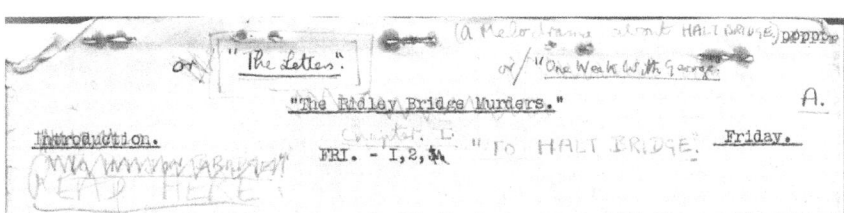

About the Author

> (a Melodrama about HALT BRIDGE) poppie
> or / "The Letter." or / "One Week With George"
>
> "The Ridley Bridge Murders." A.
>
> Introduction. Chapter 1. "TO HALT BRIDGE" Friday.
> FRI. - 1, 2, &
> READ HERE
>
> It was a Winter's evening;and with the dusk came a chill.I was cold,although I wore a thick army great-coat,but my spirits were aglow.I hurried onto the pavement out of danger from the taxis,and then into the security of the station itself.The dirty station walls,the gloomy station entrance,the wretched station officials with their slouching walk,and their unapproachable expressions,looked gay to me;people stood waiting,dejected,forlorn;soldiers packed with equipment beyond recognition staggered up the many flights of stair-cases,their boots ringing out a clatter,as they went from pillar to post misguided all the while; Air-force officers with caps at a jaunty angle,and glamourous maidens attached to crooked arms sped through the jostling crowd;everybody who moved did so in the centre of the large concrete square,about which were (amidst) clustered platforms, xxi policemen,slot-machines,and miserable passengers,or persons proposing to meet passengers g.In the centre there everyone was in a hurry,appeared to be going somewhere, yxtxx yet gave the impression of not being really certain where;their lined,worn faces turned towards the hanging notice boards,their tired eyes glxxxii glassily showed their unhappy plight.I was in England again;England had changed . There was that happy anarchy of uncertainty here,which England had never known before;convention dropped,a catastrophe for all,and all contributing towards the dirtyness,or fallen.
>
>   looked
> I looked at the tired faces;and they looked contented.I saw the waiting groups;they chattered brightly.I glanced towards the big clock;it shone ,and sparkled with a hundred dancing lights,as from a jewelled,mammoth watch.Even Newcastle station on a cold November night,when a dirty yellow mist was coming
>   was grimly
> from the Tyne outside,when all looked depressed,to me looked dazzling;I was
> home
> Home again.This was England.
>
> Shaking myself from my dreams,I walked briskly towards the ticket office ,
> apologisixxged for hitting an old man with the helmet,attached to my respirator,
>   buy my ticket,
> and lined up to make my happy purchase.After a long wait I reached the head of the
> queue
> queue,I was first;I xxxxxxxxxmade my statement;I was questioned;I answered;and I

The first page of the original manuscript

The Letters

```
19.07      -   GOVERNOR-GENERAL OF SUDAN ARRIVES IN CAIRO     -
           CAIRO, 24TH. - THE GOVERNOR-GENERAL OF THE SUDAN, MAJOR-GENERAL
SIR HUBERT HUDDLESTON, K.C.M.G., C.B., D.S.O., M.C., ARRIVED IN CAIRO
THIS AFTERNOON BY AIR FROM KHARTUM ON A SHORT VISIT TO EGYPT.
           ON ARRIVAL SIR HUBERT, WHO IS ACCOMPANIED BY LADY HUDDLESTON,
DROVE TO THE BRITISH EMBASSY, WHERE HE WILL STAY AS THE GUEST OF THE
BRITISH AMBASSADOR, SIR MILES LAMPSON.
NOV.                                       --REUTERS TICKER SERVICE.


019.30            - LONDON CLOSING EXCHANGES -        NOV. 24
(AFTER-BANK RATES)
OFFICIAL BUYER AND SELLER RATES RESPECTIVELY:-
LONDON ON:-  NEW YORK..4.02-1/2 - 4.03-1/2   BERN..17.30 - 17.40
MADRID..40.50  SELLER.
UNOFFICIAL RATES: BELGIAN CONGO..176-1/2 - 176-3/4
INDIA..1/5-31/32 - 1/6-1/32
SM                                              --RTP


19.31             - LONDON CLOSING MARKET RATES -     NOV. 24
           3 MONTHS' BANK BILLS..1-1/32% - 1-1/16%
SM                                              --RTP


19.33             - LONDON CLOSING COMMODITIES -      NOV. 24
COTTONSEED CAKES (ENGLISH MADE)           SPOT:  27-7/8  (X)
EGYPTIAN COTTON OIL CRUDE:                SPOT:  31/1-1/2 (XX)
MAIZE, LA PLATA, SHIPMENT (N.C.)          NOV:   13/10-1/2
SUGAR, WEST INDIAN, CRYSTALLISED:         SPOT:  UNQUOTED.
(X)   OFFICIAL GOVERNMENT SELLING PRICE FOR THE TRADE.
(XX)  PER CWT. GOVERNMENT SELLING PRICE FOR THE TRADE.
SM                                              --RTP


19.36      - REUTERS U.K. DAILY STAPLE COMMODITY PRICE INDEX -  NOV. 24
```

The reverse of the first page of the original manuscript

OTHER BOOKS BY PETER CARPMAEL:

WAS THERE EVER SEEN SUCH VILLAINY ?

'When he straightens up, he notices for the first time a curious green glow, which constantly varies in intensity. He gazes at the oscillating light and listens to the alternate boom and splash of water which is drumming about him. Then, surprised, he recognises the sound of the sea. Even as he realises this, in his waking consciousness, he is overtaken by a moment of panic. The tide. The tide is coming in.

'Another heavy wave from beyond lifts the water level inside and fills the cave with a pressurised gurgling, followed by a powerful, repeated boom as the pursuing waves break against the headland. This louder noise brings with it a flash of perception; he sees precisely the hopelessness of his situation. As a result of his decision to enter the cave earlier that day, he knows that he is trapped. The water continues to rise, and there is no way of escape.'

Unknown to Harry Guest, his apparently hopeless predicament is to lead him into a mysterious encounter in which a long-concealed secret reaches out across three centuries and touches the present with tragic consequences. . .

Available in ebook and paperback from Amazon Kindle

THE MAGIC CHATTY

'All about echoed the wild baying of the hounds; and above this a new noise came crashing to his ears. It was the thud of hundreds of savage dogs smashing their way towards the well with a muffled pounding, like the deep drub of native drums. There was the crackle and snap of breaking wood as the animals, crying madly, threw themselves into the glade with a last screaming crescendo more terrible than the worst nightmare that Peter had ever experienced; but he never saw the hounds. Before they came tramping and baying round, he clasped the rope inside the well with both hands, swinging his legs at the same time out into the black cavity.

'As the full weight of his body swung onto the rope, it began to unwind faster and faster with an accompanying screech from the rusty winch. Down he plunged into the well at speed with a squeak and whine from the fast baling rope, a bruising bump or two as his body thudded against the slimy wet sides, the inky darkness, the howling dogs fast receding far above, and the terror of the unknown below …'

Another chance to visit the Fairyland of Algeria, but in a parallel universe where things are subtly different from the world of Upon the Other Side !

Available in ebook, paperback and hardback from Amazon Kindle

UPON THE OTHER SIDE

'His knees trembled as he raised himself. He felt weak and sick, and his head ached. Gradually through the pain and nausea came the realisation that he had simply escaped death to fall literally into a trap, from which there was no apparent way out: if he did not find an opening somewhere, he would starve. The horror of this thought helped to clear his mind. Groping at the surrounding walls of the well, he fingered the stones carefully; they were slimy, impossible to climb, but the damp and aged mortar had fallen out in many places.

'All the time he listened intently to the babbling water, which

Other Books by Peter Carpmael

he had first noticed in the cavern. Water — how could water help him? The steady rush was louder than it had been above, which meant that it was nearer. Stepping closer to the wall, he felt for the first time that his feet were damp, for the bottom of the well was covered by stagnant slime several inches deep; it was very wet.

'Overcome by dizziness, he rested and thought. In this land of natural freaks, there might conceivably be an underground stream, surging around Mount Terror and discharging into the West gorge. If so the current could be very strong, the water pressure high …. one thought followed another and became a dangerous idea. He touched the walls again, until he reached the loose stone, which was to be the pivot of his vague but growing plan. Grasping the stone firmly, he worked it slowly back and forth between his fingers, till it began to slip freely. With a heave he forced the stone to crash down near his toes. Breathing heavily, he got up, and plunged his excited hand into the cavity. A small flow of water ran out and dripped over the walls. The two stones on either side of the new hole and the stones above were all much easier to move now. He tugged at the top stone, which gave way slowly, steadily…

'Can John find a way out of the deep well into which he has been thrown ? And can he find a way to overcome the dreaded Leader and his Orman henchmen ?

Time to read 'Upon The Other Side' !

Printed in Great Britain
by Amazon